Light up  My Life In Texas

A Novel

Connie Lewis Leonard

Garcon Publishing

Light up My Life in Texas
Published by Garcon Publishing Company
Copyright 2018, by Connie Lewis Leonard

ISBN- 13: 978-1985880405

ISBN- 10: 1985880407

This story is a work of fiction. Characters and events are the product of the author's imagination. However, inspiration for the character Winn Timberman came from the linemen of Comanche Electric Cooperative Association, the unsung heroes who light up our lives.

Scriptures are taken from the Holy Bible:
THE HOLY BIBLE, NEW INTERNATIONAL VERSION®, NIV®
Copyright © 1973, 1978, 1984, 2011 by Biblica®. Used with permission.

This book is dedicated to my Lord and Savior, Jesus Christ, whose redeeming love is unconditional and eternal.

Heartfelt appreciation goes to my husband, family, and friends who have encouraged and supported me throughout life and my writing journey.

I am thankful for the many learning opportunities through American Christian Fiction Writers, the DFW/ACFW Ready Writers, North Texas Christian Writers, ClassSeminars, and Jerry Jenkins Christian Writers Guild. A special thanks to Granbury Writers' Bloc as we have learned and developed our writing skills together.

I am grateful for special friends who critiqued this novel, catching errors and offering feedback: Lyn Goodgion, Marilyn Hayworth, Linda Manning, Connie Newsom, and Connie Youngblood.

"For you were once darkness, but now you are light in the Lord. Live as children of light."

Ephesians 5:8

New International Version

Chapter One

Andrea looked out the window of her veterinarian clinic and watched hail pummel the lineman hanging on the utility pole. Ominous, black clouds obscured the sunlight. She wondered how the man could see what he was doing with the dim light on his helmet. She wondered how long the batteries in her flashlight would hold out. How long would this storm last?

The weather alert bleeped on her phone. The tornado watch had just been upgraded to a tornado warning headed in her direction. With 90 mile an hour winds, it could strike within twenty minutes. She opened the door and clutched onto the porch pillar. Shining her light at the lineman, she yelled at him to come down. He made no move. She brandished the flashlight, motioning for him to come inside. While fighting against the wind to keep her balance, she shuffled one foot at a time until she reached the pole.

Cupping her hands she yelled, "Come down! A tornado is coming!" He stared down at her. "Tor-na-do!" She made a swirling motion with one arm with her other arm wrapped around the pole. "Tor-na-do! Come down, now!" She gestured again for him to climb down. She started to make her way back to the building. Blown forward, she hit the pillar with a thud. Holding tight she beckoned to

5

the crazy man on the pole. Once she reached the door, she turned to see him making his descent. Even with the ropes tied around his waist, the wind whipped him back and forth.

Hitting the ground, he worked to unleash the ropes before running to the door. It took both of them working together to slam and lock it. She pulled him by the arm and said, "Come on. The supply closet off the operating room should be the safest place here."

Closing the door of the large closet, Andrea shined her light in the man's face and asked, "What were you doing out there?"

"I was doing my job, trying to restore power to light up your life."

Why do all good-looking guys always have to be cocky? "Why would you want to do such a dangerous job?"

"It's an important job. Somebody has to do it."

She shook her head. "There are lots of important jobs that somebody has to do. Why a lineman?"

"Why do you work in a veterinarian clinic?" Now he shook his head. "According to an article I read in *Forbes* magazine, animal care worker is considered a more dangerous job than a lineman, which is in the top twenty."

He reads Forbes? "That's crazy. Animals aren't dangerous if you know how to treat them." She pulled two bottles of water from the box on the floor and offered him one.

He took a big swig. "Thanks." Screwing the lid back on the bottle, he said, "Electricity isn't dangerous if you know how to handle it with respect." His stomach growled. "Do you have anything to eat? I missed lunch and dinner."

"How could you think about food at a time like this?"

"I hate to break it to you, but we could be here a while."

Looking at her watch she said, "We have less than ten minutes until the tornado is supposed to hit. Think it's safe to make a run for the break room?"

He stood and pulled her to her feet. "Lead the way."

Andrea ran through the operating room and down the hall and pulled trash bags from under the cabinet. She handed one to the lineman. "You unload the fridge, and I'll get the other stuff."

"Yogurt? All you have is yogurt?"

"There are fruits and vegetables in the crisper trays." She headed toward the door. "Stop complaining and come on."

He removed his rain-soaked slicker as soon as she closed the door of the large supply closet. She sat on the blankets spread on the floor. The wind roared and hail hammered the metal roof above them.

"This sounds pretty intense." Glancing at the Australian shepherd in the back of the closet, he asked, "Is that dog dead?"

"No, she's sedated. Thankfully she's the only animal here."

"My name's Winn Timberman, and you are?"

"Andrea Travis." Her voice sounded as shaky as the walls around them. Fear swirled through her and she shivered. She hated feeling helpless, powerless. Being locked in a supply closet, with a stranger, during a tornado, was a situation beyond her control.

"Okay, Andrea." When a clap of thunder exploded, he sat down and pulled her close. She jerked to pull away, but he pulled tighter. "I'm not being fresh. I'm bigger and stronger than you. I'm just trying to shield you in case things start flying around us."

She held a large dog bed over their heads. The wind roared like a freight train. It howled like spirits of the dead. Andrea said, "I think we should pray."

"Go ahead if it makes you feel better." She could only hear him because his mouth was against her ear. Too close.

"It does make me feel better." She closed her eyes and prayed out loud, "LORD, You are my light and my salvation. LORD, you are the strength of my life. I will not be afraid. I trust You to deliver me." She knew God would hear her whether Winn could or not.

The rumbling increased. Instead of a train, it sounded like a rushing waterfall, roaring rapids, like the sky opened up and dumped an ocean of water on the dry West Texas plains. She felt trapped, smothered. In her mind she repeated the twenty-third Psalm and wondered if they would survive this valley of the shadow of death. The walls shook. Furniture crashed and banged against the building. It sounded like a demolition derby. Supplies slid off the shelves at the back of the closet.

"It's okay. We're going to be okay." He spoke into her ear drowning out the distressing sounds with his hissing breath.

"Oh, Lord, please protect us and my family." She felt crushed by the strong arms around her, but she also felt protected, like a delicate butterfly wrapped in a cocoon. She recoiled as something thudded against the door.

Winn tightened his hold and scooted to position himself between her and the sound.

"It will be okay. I've got you."

It sounded like the building was collapsing around them, but the walls of the closet stood firm. The reinforced metal door, designed to protect the drugs, held fast.

The air felt dense, stifling, suffocating. Andrea began to hyperventilate. Winn rubbed his hand up and down her arm. "Breathe deep, slow, and easy. We're going to be okay." His breath in her ear and on her neck made her feel awkward. If she had to be in this situation, why couldn't it be with someone she knew and cared about—but there was no one outside of her family.

Something beat against the door and she jerked. What if they were trapped in here? She started to stand, but he held onto her. "Stay down. We're safe in here."

***

An eternity passed. The howling stopped. As the rain pelted the roof, it reverberated off the tin like cannon shots. Andrea waved the flashlight searching for her cell phone. "Oh, great! The battery's dead."

"I left my cell phone in the truck." He walked to the door and tried to open it. He leaned against it and shoved, but it wouldn't budge. "Must be something wedged against it."

Andrea pushed on the door until her feet slid out from under her.

He laughed. "You weigh what, a hundred pounds? How do you think you're going to open it if I can't?"

She gritted her teeth. "This is not funny. What are we going to do?"

"I think we should relax, eat something, and wait to be rescued." He started digging in the plastic bags they brought from the break room. "I think we should eat the yogurt first before it ruins. The granola bars and fruit will last for a while."

"I don't expect to be here that long. My family will come looking for me."

Winn sat on the floor and began eating yogurt with a plastic spoon. "Tell me about your family. It will help pass the time."

"My parents and my two grandfathers own the T-C Quarter Horse Ranch. Maybe you've heard about it."

He nodded. "Everybody in West Texas has heard of it."

"My older brother is Brooks Travis. He used to be the backup singer and guitar player for Canada Jones, the Country Music Entertainer of the year a couple years ago. Now he's married to Katie Kane. Her parents own the Kane Cattle Ranch. Brooks sings at the Cowboy Church and writes songs for Canada Jones and other entertainers. My older sister, Celina, is married to a military man, and they're in Germany right now." She opened a yogurt. "Now it's your turn."

He opened another yogurt. "My story is not as impressive as yours."

"Everybody's story is important because everyone is important, created by God, in His image, for a specific purpose."

"So you're real religious?"

"No, I'm not *real religious.* I'm a Christian." She finished her yogurt and set it aside. "Your turn to talk."

"My dad was Stony Timberman, the world champion bull rider. His name was actually Stephen, but he called himself Stony after some old TV character."

"Winn is a unique name. Are you named after anyone?"

"No, my dad thought if he named me Winn that'd make me a winner." He set the yogurt aside and drank some water. "How do you eat this stuff?"

"It's nutritious, low-fat, and quick and easy when I'm on the go." She polished an apple on her sleeve. "If I eat a light breakfast and lunch, I can indulge at dinner, especially when I eat with my family. My mom is an excellent cook." She paused, trying to make eye contact, but Winn was eating a granola bar. "You spoke of your dad in past tense."

"Yeah." He swallowed and took another drink of water. "He rode bulls and was never hurt much. He began buying stock to raise bucking bulls. Then he was gored by a cantankerous old brahma." He cleared his voice. "Nobody was around at the time, so he bled to death."

11

She put her hand on his arm. "I am truly sorry."

"Yeah, well, time goes on." He gazed into her deep blue eyes, stared at her lips, and refocused on her eyes. "So, you married or anything?"

She fidgeted and lowered her head. "No. I just graduated from vet school at A&M. I didn't have time for a social life while I was in school."

"You're a vet? I heard Doc Mitchell retired."

"Yes, I interned with him a couple of summers. He's a great guy. His arthritis and back problems made it too painful for him to continue to practice. Do you raise bulls now?" She bit into the apple.

He shook his head, "No, my mom sold all of them after my dad died. She kept a few heifers, one old tame bull, and a couple of horses. I was only 16, so I didn't have any say about it."

"How did you become a lineman for the county co-op?" She wiped her hands on her jeans and continued without waiting for his answer. "My family sings old country songs. My Grandfather Abuelo sings that old song 'Wichita Lineman' better than Glenn Campbell ever did."

"It must be old because I haven't heard it."

"Oh it's a great song, short, simple, and to the point, about an ordinary guy, an unsung hero, thinking about the girl he loves while working as a lineman, a telephone lineman actually." She closed her eyes and put her hand over her heart. "Glenn Campbell did an amazing job on the guitar."

"Hmm. I think if I ever heard it, I'd remember it."

"When we get out of here, I'll invite you to my family's ranch for a barbeque and an old fashioned singing—classic country is all they sing. I'll make my famous melt-in-your-mouth chocolate cake with fudgy icing, and Gramps will make homemade ice cream. I'll ask my grandfather Abeulo to sing it for you."

"Sounds like a deal. Lineman wasn't my first choice, but that's another story." He finished the granola bar and took another drink of water. "You're shivering." He wrapped his arms around her and pulled her close. He let go when she stiffened. "It's okay. I'm not going to hurt you. I'm one of the good guys, a public servant and all that."

"I should have grabbed some more dog blankets, but I was doing laundry when the power went out."

"We can keep each other warm." His clicked on his radio. "This is Winn Timberman. Come in." The only response was static. "They'll come looking for me when this passes over. The co-op keeps close tabs on their employees. We're a brotherhood and take care of each other."

"My family will come, too, as soon as it's safe." Sitting beside him, she tried to relax, but her heart beat out a staccato pattern.

***

Andrea's stomach growled, and she looked at her watch. "It's 7:30. We've been here over an hour. How long do you think it will be before they come for us?"

"It depends on how much debris is on the roads. If there's flooding and downed power lines, it will make it more dangerous. Our guys will be out working on the lines. The county and state police will be working through the night."

"You think we'll have to stay here all night?" She shivered at the thought and flipped off the flashlight.

"We're safe in here. We have water and food, well sort of." He laughed.

"Okay, let's keep talking to pass the time. What is your favorite food?"

"Meat." He laughed and deepened his voice, "Men like meat."

"Okay, what kind of meat?"

"Steak, brisket, ribs, hamburgers. What do you like besides yogurt?" His breath brushed her hair, and she cringed.

"Mexican food. My mom makes the best. I love sweets, so baking is my specialty."

"I can't wait for that barbeque and singing, especially the chocolate cakes you were talking about."

"We'll do it soon." She inhaled deeply. "You asked if I was married or anything. What about you." She felt his body tense.

The lull stilled the air before he answered, "I'm unattached."

She stood up. "My legs are stiff from sitting on the floor. I think I'll move a little."

He stretched and stood also. "Yeah, I'm not used to sitting around." In the darkness he bumped into her. She stumbled

14

backwards, and he wrapped his arms around her. "Sorry I didn't mean to knock you over."

His cheek brushed hers. She stepped back. "That's okay." She knelt on her hands and knees and fumbled to turn on the flashlight. Feeling the blush in her face, she hoped he couldn't see it. "Let's leave the light on while we're up so we don't bump into each other again." She did a few neck rolls and Yoga stretches until she noticed him monitoring her moves. "If I turn the flashlight off, will you stay put until I work some of the kinks out?"

His twinkling blue-gray eyes reflected the light. His smile spread across his face like honey on a hot biscuit. "You don't have to turn the light off. I'll sit down."

Her heart pounded. Her palms felt sweaty. The air felt stuffy. "Do you think we could run out of air and suffocate in here?"

"No, no way." He stooped in front of the door. "There's air coming in. Here, feel."

"Move out of the way." He obliged and she knelt. Putting her face on the floor, she inhaled deeply. Sitting up, she leaned against the door, her head on her knees.

"Are you alright?" Concern etched his face as he knelt in front of her,.

She nodded, taking deep breaths to regain her composure. "I think I just got up and moved too fast after sitting for so long. Can you turn off the flashlight. We may need the light later on."

"Sure." Shuffling his feet, he said, "I would hate a job where I had to sit inside all day, in front of a computer, or talking on the phone. Being a lineman, being outside, somewhere and something different every day is much more to my liking."

Not trusting her voice, she didn't respond.

"Look, I'm sorry if I embarrassed or offended you." He cleared his voice. "I didn't mean to stare, but you are good looking."

"Men," she puffed, "are so shallow."

"I don't think it's shallow to admire beauty,'' he paused, "like a beautiful purple and pink sunrise on the Texas plains. The red and gold of the sunset. Wild flowers in the spring. The smell of fresh cut grass. And babies—baby calves and baby horses, puppies and kittens, baby birds newly hatched, and real babies." His voice lowered to a husky whisper. "We think about life and death and love." His stomach rumbled, and he laughed. "Right now I'm thinking about that barbeque, chocolate cake, and ice cream."

Fighting back tears, she said, "I'm thinking about my family and wondering if they're alright."

"We just have to hope for the best. That's what I'm doing, hoping my family is okay. You prayed about trusting God, so don't worry." He picked up the flashlight and switched it back on. He opened the trash bag. "You want an apple or something?"

He found a jar of peanut butter and opened it up. "Almost as good as meat," he said sniffing. Pulling a knife out of his pocket, he cut up the apple, and spread each piece with peanut butter. "You want some?" he asked, waving the knife.

"No, thanks."

He finished the apple and tossed it in their trash bag. "How long have you been doing yoga?"

"I took it as a P.E. elective in college. The stretches help me relax and wind down. I don't do the weird New Age meditation stuff."

"And it helps you stay in shape," he said.

"Have you ever done yoga?"

He scowled. "No way." His lips turned up in a mischievous grin. "There's nothing wrong with it, for a girl, I mean, but it's not for me."

"What do you do to stay in shape, for a guy, I mean?"

He stood erect, chest out, shoulders back, stomach in. "I work. As a lineman, I get a pretty good workout climbing poles, trudging through pastures and climbing fences to get to the poles, dodging dogs, and playing ring-around-the-rosy with cantankerous old cows."

"Okay, I have to hear that story."

"Once I was following the line, trying to find the problem. I came across an old mama cow who thought I was trespassing just a little too close to her baby. She took off after me. The only shelter was a scrawny mesquite tree. I hid behind it, but she came running around that tree after me." He leaned forward, moving his head from side to side. "We were playing ring-around-the-rosy when my partner came up and distracted her with his rope. I got my rope out, and with both of us swinging our loops, we were able to chase her off."

Andrea laughed until her sides hurt. "I would love to see that."

"Gotta little mean streak, do ya?"

"You laughed, too."

"It is funny now, but it wasn't then." He tilted his head and flashed her a friendly grin. "Besides, laughing's better than crying."

"You're right." She dabbed at her eyes. "Do you have any more funny stories?"

"When I was in high school, I thought I might try my hand at bullfighting. I was out there prancing around in that arena. When the rider got bucked off, the bull went after him. I did my job and got in between them. That bull lowered his head and came after me. I jumped for the fence but not before he snagged my baggy britches and ripped 'em off." He slid his hands down his thighs, pushing his jeans over his boots. "It was pretty embarrassing for a sixteen-year-old boy to have his red long johns exposed to everyone at the county fair, especially since they had a hole in the cheek."

"I can see it all now." She felt herself blush. "I mean, I can imagine how embarrassing that would be."

"Now it's your turn to tell a funny story."

"I'm pretty serious, and I'm not a big risk taker."

"Ah, come on. You're a vet who just opened your own clinic. I think that's taking a risk."

She stretched her legs, crossing her ankles. "You're right. I just hope there's enough insurance to cover the damage, including the horse trailer, pickup, and the living quarters horse trailer out back that

18

belongs to my dad. He loaned it to me since he's retired."

He sat next to her and said, "Don't worry until you know you have something to worry about." When she scooted away, he stood up. "So Dustin Travis is your dad?"

"Yes. You've heard of him?"

"He's one of the best ropers who ever lived. I've seen him work his magic with a rope."

"He retired because of his health, but he's doing better now. He was a wanderer, always on the road, but now he's home taking a more active part in the ranch. He has a couple of roping clinics scheduled for this summer."

He paced. "That's good. It's hard to give up something you love." She detected a hint of sorrow in his voice, but she didn't want to ask, didn't want anything else weighing on her mind.

Chapter Two

After what seemed an eternity, a vehicle horn shattered the silence. "They're here! Someone's here to rescue us!" Andrea stood up and beat on the door. "In here! We're in here!"

"Save your breath. If the roof or part of the building collapsed, it will take them a while to make their way in here," he said calmly. "The co-op knows where I was working. They'll keep looking." He retrieved the flashlight and positioned it so the light would shine under the door. "Just take some deep breaths, relax, and listen."

She heard banging, barking, and then voices—her dad and grandfathers. "Andrea!" She knelt down and stuck her fingers under the door. "In here. We're in here." The banging and scraping intensified before she heard a strange voice say, "Winn, you in there?"

He face lit up. "Keith, in here." He moved the flashlight back and forth as a signal.

"Okay, buddy. It'll take a while to get the roof away from the door. Just hang tight."

"Are you alright, Andrea?" Her dad's voice boomed, joined by barking.

"I'm fine, Dad, now that you're here," She shouted. "Hey,

Peppy."

Chain saws revved up. "They're cutting away the debris. Let's back up." Winn pulled her to the back of the supply closet.

Andrea squatted in front of the Australian shepherd. She rubbed her hands along the dog's side. "She's still in La La Land. We may have to carry her out."

"What's wrong with her?"

"She was bitten by a rattlesnake. Her breathing and heart rate are good. She should be fine. I brought her in here and sedated her when the weather turned bad."

"She's a beautiful Aussie," Winn said, patting her on the head.

"She's a champion cow dog named Bleu Neva. Her pups go for $500.00 and up. We have bred our dog Peppy with her a couple of times."

"We have a Catahoula-heeler cross named Clyde. He's fearless." He shook his head. "Then my mom has a puffball named Fluffy."

"What kind of dog is Fluffy?"

"She's Peekapoo, Pekingnese and Poodle—a little yelper."

The walls shook around them. Winn grabbed the large dog bed and held it over their heads. Bits of sheetrock and insulation rained down on them. He shielded her with his body. They heard a truck engine rev up followed by a loud crash, a clatter of metal, scraping noises, and cheers.

The door opened, and Andrea leaped into her father's arms.

He wrapped her in a bear hug until she sputtered. "Ugh! I can't breathe." Her father stepped back and her two grandfathers took turns hugging her. Peppy leaped on her and then walked over to sniff Bleu Neva.

Keith stuck his head in the door. "Winn, you okay?"

Andrea moved out of the doorway, and Winn walked out of the closet. His fellow lineman grabbed his hand and slapped his shoulder. "Man, we were worried about you being out in the middle of nowhere when the storm hit."

"Good thing for me Andrea invited me in for dinner."

Andrea could feel herself blush. Then her eyes took in the devastation. The entire front of her clinic was demolished. She couldn't hold back the tears. "Just look at this mess."

Her dad wrapped an arm around her. "The important thing is that you're okay."

Her Gramps said, "If it can be fixed with money, don't worry about it."

Defeat squeezed the breath out of her. "I don't have the money to fix it."

Abuelo said, "Who needs money? Our Nieta is safe. We are happy."

"Have you seen my pickup and trailer and your living quarters' trailer?" she asked her dad. "They were parked out back."

"We can look at them tomorrow in the daylight. Right now we need to get you home to your mama. She's been trying to call you for hours." He led her through the rubble.

"My cell phone died." She felt for the phone in her pocket and turned back toward the closet. "Wait, I have to get the dog. She's sedated, so we'll have to carry her."

"I'll get her," Gramps said.

Andrea turned to Winn and extended her hand. "Thanks for keeping me company, for helping me stay calm, and for trying to protect me."

He shook her hand and smiled. "Thanks for sharing the closet and your food."

"Do you have a card or something so I can call and invite you to dinner?" She asked.

He shook his head. "If you can give me one of your cards, I'll call you."

She hesitated, but since her business number was already public, she pulled a business card from the holder in her pocket and handed him one. Turning her back to him, she locked the closet door. "I'll have to move the drugs to a safe place in the morning."

***

The next morning Andrea woke to the spicy smell of sausage and chili. Her muscles ached, stiff from sitting on the floor in the supply closet for hours. She wanted to stay under the covers, safe in her childhood bedroom, safe from the devastation of the tornado. She'd have to check with her insurance company to have the damage assessed, to see what would be covered and what wouldn't. *Get up,*

23

get your big girl britches on, and go to work.

After a long, hot shower, Andrea stepped into an empty dining room. Her mother stood at the kitchen sink. "Your father and grandfathers are out working. The tornado took out a large section of fence along the north pasture bordering the highway. The men were able to get the horses into the barn, so the fence is the only damage we suffered."

Andrea forced a smile. "I'm thankful my family is safe. I prayed for you all while I was in that closet."

Her mother hugged her. "We were in touch with Brooks and Katie, who were in contact with her family, and we all prayed together. The Kanes lost part of their fence, also. Brooks is at their ranch helping with repairs." She opened the oven. "Sit, and I'll bring your breakfast."

"Mom, I don't think I feel like eating." Her stomach swirled like the tornado.

"You need to eat before you face the day. I'll call your father when you're finished and he'll take you to your clinic."

She shrugged. "What's left of it."

Carmella hugged her daughter. "The sun is shining. The dust is settled. Today is a new beginning."

"Or the end of my dreams." Andrea shook her head.

"Dreams don't die unless you give up on them." She pulled out a chair. "Sit. I made chili and tortillas for huevos rancheros. All I have to do is cook your eggs." Standing at the stove she asked, "Do you want milk or hot tea?"

"Both, I guess."

***

Driving to the clinic, Dustin tapped on the steering wheel. "Don't be too upset when you see things. You have insurance on the pickup, and I kept the insurance on the living quarters' horse trailer. The clinic can be rebuilt."

The knot in her stomach tightened. "You saw them last night? How bad is it, Dad?"

"I'm not an adjuster, but I imagine they're totaled." He paused. "Do you have insurance on the old trailer you got from Doc Mitchell?"

"I think so. The policy is in the safe in the supply closet." She rested her arm on the door, her cheek in her hand. "Hopefully some of the equipment can be recovered. I'll have to move the meds to a safe place so some druggie doesn't try to steal them."

"You can stay at home until the clinic is rebuilt. Maybe practice from there. You could use the apartment in the barn, or we could even get a portable building for you to use as a clinic, if that will help."

She dug deep into her reservoir of courage. "Thanks, Dad. Let's just take one step at a time. The first thing will be to contact the insurance agent and see where to go from there."

***

After calling the insurance adjuster, Andrea loaded the drugs and surgical instruments in the back seat of her father's pickup. "It's a good thing the storage space in your living quarters' trailer is small. Most of my clothes and personal belongings are still in my room at home."

"When did the adjuster say he would get out here?" Dustin asked as he surveyed the destruction.

"He said they're prioritizing homes before businesses, so it will probably be next week. He told me to secure what I could, but other than what's in the closet, it doesn't look like much is salvageable." She jumped when her phone beeped. "Hello . . . Yes, this is Dr. Travis . . . Hold on." Pressing the phone against her chest she whispered, "Dad, can you take me on a call to the Rocking Z Ranch?"

"Sure, if you're up to it."

She nodded. "I'll be there in about twenty minutes." She hung up and said to her dad, "You ready for vet tech training?"

"I've done my share of doctoring horses and cattle in my time. In the early days, we didn't have money to call a vet unless it was life or death." He opened the passenger door of his pickup for her.

At the Rocking Z Ranch, she treated a couple of horses suffering from cuts and scrapes. A prize bull couldn't be saved. She received another call from a family whose dog had a broken leg. She told them she would meet them at the T-C Quarter Horse Ranch.

"Dad, I think we could use the apartment in the barn as a

clinic. I could use the kitchen and restroom. We could move out the furniture and put in an exam table, when I can get one. And maybe I could use a couple of stalls if I need to treat any horses. I probably need to invest in a couple of portable kennels, too."

"You order whatever you need, and I'll pay for it. You can pay me back when you get your insurance money."

She turned and looked out the side window. "If I don't get enough from the insurance, I may have to take out a long-term loan to rebuild."

"You know your grandfathers, your mother and I, and Brooks will help you. That's what family is all about."

She patted her dad on the shoulder. "I know, and that's why I love you so much."

He cleared his throat. "We have to protect our interests. I don't want any animals in our barn that could infect our horses. That's our livelihood."

"I won't bring any animals in that could be contagious. Our horses are worth more than my clinic and everything in it."

***

After examining the dog, she told the owners, "I know the leg is broken, but without an x-ray, I can't be sure how bad it is. I can't operate here, not yet, but I can try to set it and put a splint on it. The other option is to take him to a vet in Lubbock."

"Things are real bad at our place. We don't really have the money or the time to take him to Lubbock. How much will it cost for you to try to fix it? Our kids love this old dog."

Andrea saw the pain in the man's tired eyes. She knew it wasn't just the kids who loved the dog. "Let me do what I can now, and we'll work something out later about the payment."

She set the dog's leg, put a splint on it, gave him some pain meds, and sent him home with his family.

After they left, Andrea leaned against the wall of the apartment. She felt a sense of accomplishment, renewed hope and determination. "Dad, I know this is what God created me to do—to be a vet. I've always loved animals and wanted to take care of them."

Her father rolled his shoulders. "Yes, every bird with a broken wing and the frog that went through the washer of hot bleach water."

She snickered. "I felt responsible for that poor frog. If I hadn't been playing with him in my room, he wouldn't have gotten wrapped up in my sheets."

Dustin Travis put his arm around her shoulders. "We're proud of you, all your hard work and studying. We'll do all we can to help get your clinic back up and running, Dr. Travis."

Her grandfathers walked in and heard the last part of the conversation. Gramps said. "We can build a bigger, better building, something that could withstand a tornado."

"Aw, Gramps, I don't need anything bigger as long as I have a sturdy supply closet, like the one that saved my life."

Abuelo said, "What can we do to help you until the building is rebuilt?"

"I can set up a temporary practice here in the barn. I'll need to clean out the apartment, just the front—I won't disturb your bedrooms. I need an exam table that can double as a surgery table, and I'll have to get an x-ray machine. I'll need transportation."

Her phone beeped. "Hello, this is Dr. Travis. . . Hold on a minute."

Before she could ask, her dad said, "I can take you wherever you need to go."

"I'll be there in twenty minutes." She hung up and squared her shoulders. "Let's go. I don't know whether to call you my vet tech or my chauffeur."

"Just call me Dad. That should cover all the bases."

"We'll have this apartment cleaned out by the time you get back," Gramps said.

"You want us to leave anything in here?" Abuelo asked.

"Just the table, chairs, and appliances." Andrea hugged her grandfathers. "Thanks."

She gave her dad directions and said, "While you're driving, I think I'll get online and order a few things."

"Let me pull over so I can get my credit card out of my wallet."

She shook her head. "I'll use my card." She pinched the bridge of her nose. "I may have to borrow from you later, depending on what the insurance doesn't cover. I may have to live at home until I'm fifty."

"I doubt that, but our home is always your home." His fingers tapped out the rhythm of the country song playing on the radio. "So, tell me about the lineman who sat out the tornado with you."

"Don't go getting any ideas. He was working on the power lines when the warning came over the radio." Shaking her head, she said, "I told him he could come to dinner at the ranch and meet my family, as payment for helping me stay calm. He's never heard Glenn Campbell's song 'Wichita Lineman'—if you can believe that."

"This younger generation doesn't know what real music is." He turned down the radio and started singing the lyrics. They both laughed.

"I'm glad Brooks got his talent from Mom and Abuelo. Celina and I were left out of the gift of music, like you."

Dustin put his hand over his heart. "You're breaking my heart."

She patted his arm. "Keep singing. I need a good laugh—it's medicine for the soul."

He sang "Achy Breaky Heart" making his voice more off tune than normal.

Chapter Three

The next week Andrea stayed busy setting up a provisional clinic in the main barn of T-C Quarter Horse Ranch. Each day people brought small pets to her. Her grandfathers allowed her to use their pickups so she could make calls to take care of livestock. She signed a contract with The Rocking Z Ranch to perform artificial insemination using the stored sperm from their prize bull that was killed in the tornado.

The good news was that her pickup had full coverage, so she was able to replace it with a new red club cab. The bad news was it would cost far more than the insurance adjuster's estimate to rebuild the clinic. Since he had retired and no longer traveled with the rodeo, her dad promised to give her the money his insurance paid for his living quarters' trailer.

One evening at dinner, Andrea announced to her family, "I've decided to go with a metal building. It'll be cheaper and quicker to put up."

Abuelo shook his head. "But Neita, we want you to be safe. Money can't replace my beautiful granddaughter."

"The bricks came tumbling down when the big bad wind blew. The metal exterior could go up in a day, and y'all could finish off the inside. I could live there if we put in a bedroom and a private bathroom with a shower. Later on, when I'm ready to move out, the vet tech could use it. I could make the kitchen in the break area larger, and the reception center could serve as my living room." She took a deep breath. "I have been doing some research, and I would like to have a safe room that could also be used as a supply closet. Texas Tech has a Debris Impact Testing program. We can get plans and specifications from them. If y'all could build that, I would be forever grateful."

"Why don't we just build you a storm cellar?" Gramps asked.

"Being underground, always gave me the creeps, and I hate spiders and snakes." Andrea shuddered. "If a tornado warning comes while I'm sleeping, I can get in the safe room without going outside." Her phone beeped.

"Can't it wait until after dinner?" her mother asked, arching her well-defined eyebrows.

Andrea shook her head and answered the phone as she stood and walked out of the dining room. "Dr. Travis."

"Hello, Andrea. This is Winn Timberman."

Her pulse raced. "Oh, hi, Winn." She paused to steady her shaky voice. "How are you doing?"

"I've been working ten- and twelve-hour days since the tornado trying to get the lines back up and the power restored."

She walked outside to the porch and sat on the swing. "My family is fortunate we didn't lose power. Thank goodness we have a

32

generator for back-up if we need it. The only damage we had was a downed fence. Besides my clinic."

"How are things going with that?"

"I've set up a make-shift clinic here at the ranch. Of course the insurance isn't paying what it will cost to rebuild and replace everything, but my family will help." She chuckled. "I may have to live here till I'm fifty to pay them back." She kicked her feet and set the swing gently rocking. "What about you? Did your family have any damage?"

"Not much. The funnel had dissipated by the time it reached here, but we had a couple of downed trees from the strong winds. We'll have plenty of firewood for the winter" He groaned. "For many winters, once I get it cut and stacked."

She stared up at the stars, thankful the sky was clear and the wind calm. "Would you like to come to dinner next Saturday? I want you to hear that Glenn Campbell song."

"I Googled it. It's a pretty good song, especially the guitar playing."

"My grandfather Abuelo, does an amazing job singing that song, sings with so much passion. My mom harmonizes perfectly with him."

"Do you sing, too?"

She shook her head. "You don't want to hear me sing or my dad or Gramps either. The musical gene comes from the Cordova side of the family, and Brooks is the only one who inherited it."

"Can I bring anything, for dinner?" He paused. "What time should I come Saturday?"

"No need to bring anything, because you're our guest. Can you make it by six?"

"Sure. I look forward to seeing you again."

She stopped the swing, but her heart continued to rock. "Okay. See you then." *A lineman for the county. An extraordinary song about an ordinary guy. Are you an ordinary guy, Mr. Winn Timberman? Or are you an unsung hero?*

***

Saturday Winn worked all day to catch up on the chores that had gone undone since the tornado. He cut up the fallen trees and stacked firewood. When he told his mother he was going out to dinner with a friend, she frowned. "Charity and I have hardly seen you since the tornado. I would like you to stay home tonight and have dinner with us."

"I'll be home all day tomorrow." He picked up his daughter and swung her around. "Who is Daddy's baby doll?"

She giggled and said, "Chari."

"I love you a bushel and a peck and a hug around the neck." He hugged her tight and kissed her golden curls. "Tomorrow is our special day. Do you want to have a picnic by the pond?"

"Can Clyde and Fluffy go with us?" Chari batted her long eyelashes at her dad.

"Only if they don't eat all our food?" He winked at her.

"What do you want to eat?"

She shrugged her slight shoulders. "Peanut butter and jelly samwiches and choc-late cupcakes?"

"Okay, but now that you're a big four-year-old, you'll need to eat some vegetables or fruit."

"Not carrots." She wrinkled her tiny, turned-up nose. "Maybe a nana?"

"You got it." He sat her down and kissed her chubby, cherubic cheek. "If I'm not home before bedtime, don't forget to say your prayers so you can have sweet dreams." He hugged his mother, and said, "Thanks, Mom. I'll be home before curfew, I promise." Faith rolled her eyes.

On the way to the T-C Quarter Horse Ranch, Winn stopped and bought chocolate cupcakes for Charity and two boxes of chocolates, one for his mother and one for Andrea. Chocolates weren't as personal as flowers. They could be for Andrea's entire family. They might sweeten his mother's mood.

***

Meeting Andrea's family, watching them, listening to their jovial banter, Winn felt awkward, like a mustang trying to join a herd of thoroughbreds. Brooks Travis seemed down-to-earth, nothing like Winn expected a country/western music star to be. His wife Katie was a cute, little brunette. Their son Austin's deep, blue eyes sparkled as he rubbed his mother's protruding belly, telling Winn that he was going to have a baby brother.

35

Andrea was a classic beauty, like her mother Carmella—black hair and astonishing violet, blue eyes. Andrea, Brooks, and Austin got their eyes from their Grandfather Cordova, Abuelo. Her father, Dustin, had gray eyes like his father Dean, Andrea's Gramps. Chari would stand out in this group with her golden blond hair and green eyes.

Dustin said, "I met your dad on the rodeo circuit. He was a great bull rider."

Winn took a drink of water. *Yeah, I'm glad he was great at something.* "Thanks. I've seen you work your magic with a rope. Andrea says you're going to be holding some roping clinics."

"Yes, I have one scheduled the week before the Fourth of July for kids and another one in October for adults."

"My Grandpa Dustin is teaching me everything he knows." Austin beamed.

The adults laughed. "He's the best student I've ever had," Dustin said, winking at his grandson.

"What about you, Brooks? Did you ever rope?" Winn asked.

"I tried, but I wasn't good enough. Music is my passion." Brooks draped his arm over his wife's shoulder. "God, my family, and music, in that order."

Andrea smiled. "You should come to the Cowboy Church and hear him sing." She escorted Winn to the round picnic table under the shade of an old oak tree. She leaned over and whispered, "Relax. They won't eat you."

Winn nodded, hoping the heat radiating up his arm where she touched him didn't show on his face. Abuelo set the sizzling brisket on the table. Brooks said grace, and the clatter of dishes and silverware combined with the chatter.

Winn inhaled the savory scents. "This brisket is the best I've ever eaten—tender and juicy, with a spicy, hot kick."

"That's my secret Mexican rub." Abuelo flashed a gap-tooth smile. "Top secret."

"If he told you what's in it, he'd have to kill you," Gramps said in his deep, serious voice.

Abuelo shrugged and nodded.

"Winn, tell us about your family," Carmella said.

"I'm an only child. I live with my mom." He didn't want to mention Charity, not yet. "We moved to West Texas when I was fourteen. My dad died when I was sixteen. My mom sold most of the bucking bulls he was raising, but we have a few head of cattle." As he watched Andrea's family talk and laugh, he wondered how it would feel to be part of a large, loving family.

Andrea cut the cake and Gramps dished up the homemade ice cream. Winn took a bite of the chocolate cake with rich, gooey, fudgy icing. The cool, creamy vanilla ice cream took the sugary edge off the chocolate.

"This is the best cake and ice cream I've ever tasted," Winn said, licking his lips.

"Andrea made the cake." Carmella beamed. "She is a great

cook."

Andrea cringed at her mother's obvious sales pitch.

***

After dinner, the family sat on the wrap-around porch. Abuelo, Carmella, and Brooks with their guitars; Katie and Austin with their violins. When Abuela sang "Wichita Lineman", Winn concurred with Andrea that it was better than Glenn Campbell's version. The family sang many other classic country songs as well as some of the contemporary songs Brooks wrote and sang with Canada Jones. The evening ended with Katie and Austin playing "Amazing Grace" on their violins. Katie's playing sounded like a heavenly orchestra, and the kid was really good for a seven-year-old.

Andrea walked Winn to his pick-up. "Thanks for coming." She gazed up at the full moon. "I can never repay you for what you did during the tornado."

"I didn't do anything." He slid his hands in his pockets.

"Yes, you did. You kept me calm while keeping me company."

"And you fed me—yogurt." He laughed. "But tonight's meal made up for that."

"Well, take care and stay safe." She backed up.

He took a step closer and said, "Would you like to go out? I think it's my turn to treat you to dinner."

Her heart flip-flopped. She wasn't ready for this. "Um, I'm going to be super busy cleaning up the mess from the tornado, making plans, and getting the new clinic up and running." She didn't want to hurt his feelings, but she didn't want to lead him on. "Thanks for the offer, though."

"I'd like to help. I'm strong." He flexed his biceps. "I'm pretty handy with a hammer and saw. I've done my fair share of community service work before."

She raised her eyebrows. "Oh, you have?"

"In my younger, wilder days. But not too wild." He smiled. "Maybe I could entertain you with some more funny stories."

"I'm not even sure when we'll start working."

"Will you call me when you do? I'd like to see you again." He stepped closer. "I would really like to get to know you better."

She stepped back. "I'm at the cowboy church every Sunday."

He nodded and opened the door to his pickup. "Well, maybe I'll see you around."

She watched him drive away. *Yeah, maybe I'll see you around.* She felt all eyes scrutinizing her as she made her way back to the porch.

"He seems like a nice young man," Carmella said, searching her daughter's face for a reaction.

"He's cute, too," Katie added.

The men stared at her, all bug-eyed, waiting for a response.

"Thanks for dinner and the music." Andrea hugged her mother and grandfathers. "It's been a long week, and I'm tired." She walked to the door. "See you in the morning."

"Humph." Gramps spit tobacco juice into the flower bed. "I guess I'll turn in, too."

"We need to go so Austin can take a bath before bed." The boy frowned at his mother's statement..

Brooks stood and said, "Let's go, Pardner. Church comes early in the morning."

After everyone left, Carmella asked her husband, "What do you think?"

"I think dinner was great."

Sitting next to him on the swing, she said, "You know what I mean. About Andrea?"

"I think she's over twenty-one, smart, and sassy."

Carmella nuzzled her husband's neck. "What do you think about Winn?"

"He seems okay. His dad was a rounder, but so was I once upon a time." He kissed his wife on the cheek. "Don't worry about Andrea. She's got a good head on her shoulders. She can take care of herself."

Chapter Four

Winn told himself to forget about Andrea. She was a thoroughbred. He was a mangy mustang. She had a family who loved her. He had a daughter. Charity was his sunshine, and he loved her with all his heart. He also had a mom who needed him, despite her compulsive controlling ways. He had a job and responsibilities to keep the home place going. He had given up his dream to be a bull rider, but one day he hoped to fulfill his dad's dream of raising bucking bulls.

The more he told himself not to think about Andrea, the more she invaded his thoughts. Driving down the highway, he pictured those deep blue eyes, black hair, creamy complexion, and perfect body. But she was more than just a pretty face. She stood out from the crowd. She had a gentle strength, character and integrity, intelligence and common sense, an easy laugh. He hadn't felt this way about a woman since Janae. Three years ago, after the car accident, he didn't think he would ever be interested in another woman. Andrea personified innocence and virtue.

His heart was still an open wound. Sometimes he wondered if it would ever heal, ever be whole, if he could ever love again. He thought of Andrea and wondered what it would be like to hold her hand, to hug her, to kiss her, to tell her his deepest thoughts, to share his daughter with her. Charity was a mini version of Janae, golden-blond hair, green eyes, cute little turned up nose, the same sweet smile with one dimple on her right cheek.

***

One day he drove by Andrea's clinic on his way home from work. There she was working alongside her family, clearing debris and loading it on a flatbed trailer. Before he could talk himself out of it, Winn whipped his truck into the drive. He parked, took a deep breath, and ambled up to her. "Hey, it looks like you're making headway."

She removed a glove and extended her hand. "It's good to see you. Are you still working late every night?"

"Actually, I was on my way home and saw y'all out here, so I thought I'd stop and see how you're doing."

She removed her other glove. "Would you like some water or tea? I need a little break."

"Water sounds good." He winked. "And maybe a yogurt if you have one."

She giggled. "Too late. I ate mine for lunch." She handed him a bottle of water and swiped her bottle on her jeans. "My mom should be bringing dinner in a little while if you'd like to stay and eat with us. We're trying to get as much done as possible so the new plumbing can be installed and the foundation extended. The next priority will be the safe room, and then the metal exterior."

"Dinner sounds good, but only if I can stay and help."

She tilted her head as in deep thought. "Okay. We can use an extra pair of hands."

"Let me call my mom so she won't wait on me."

***

Andrea watched him as he talked on the phone. She couldn't hear what he said, but she thought it was a plus that he was thoughtful enough to call his mother. That didn't mean she was interested in him as anything more than a friend, if that much.

She noticed her dad, brother, and grandfathers watching her and Winn as they worked side-by-side, but they kept their distance. When her mother arrived, they washed their hands with water from a jug and sat in lawn chairs to eat burritos, watermelon, and snickerdoodle cookies.

"The burritos and cookies are delicious. Thank you, Mrs. Travis." Winn was cordially polite to her mother, but Andrea wondered why he clammed up around the men. "I better be going. I have some things I need to do at home."

Carmella smiled. "Thank you, Winn. Would you like to take some cookies home? We have plenty."

He looked uncertain, but then he nodded. Carmella handed him the plastic bag. "Oh, I can't take all of them, just a couple."

"I made a big batch. We have plenty at home to snack on. Please, take them."

"Well, okay." He accepted the bag and turned to go. "Maybe

I'll see you tomorrow."

Andrea walked him to his truck. "Thanks for the help. I understand you have other responsibilities, so please don't feel obligated to come here."

The muscles in his face relaxed. "I like spending time with you." He smiled. "Maybe you'll go out to dinner with me when you find out I'm an okay guy."

She felt the knot in her stomach tighten. Avoiding his gaze, she said, "I already think you're an okay guy." She looked at his face, a boyishly handsome face. "I'm just not going to have any time to date for a while."

"Did I say date?" He flashed that ready smile. "You have to eat. I have to eat. We could eat together, sometime."

"Sometime." She walked away but turned to wave when she heard his truck start. She threw her water bottle in the trash bag. "Are we ready to get back to work?" Her family stared at her. "What?"

"He doesn't talk much," Gramps put a dip of tobacco in his mouth, "at least not to us."

"Maybe he's shy," Carmella said.

"Maybe he's got a guilty conscience," Gramps mumbled through his bulging lips.

"A guilty conscience about what?" Andrea's voice sounded sharp.

Brooks laughed. "Look at the fire flashing in those eyes."

"Don't tease your little sister." Carmella pointed her finger at her son.

"She may be little, but you better watch your step. She might use some of that Karate stuff to take you down," Dustin said.

Brooks grabbed his sister and wrapped his arms around her. She flipped him on the ground and put her knee on his throat. "Say uncle!" He gasped, so she moved her knee. When she offered her hand to help him up, he pulled her down beside him and tickled her. She kicked her leg, knocked him over, and sat on his chest. "Things have changed since we were kids. If you don't behave, I may hog tie you with my black belt."

"Okay. Uncle! I give!" he howled.

She walked away leaving him on his back in the dirt.

"Told ya," Dustin drawled.

Brooks stood and knocked the dust off his pants. "Somebody better warn Winn."

Andrea turned, her eyes flashing. "Don't you dare!"

"He at least needs to know about your spitfire temper."

"Brooks, mind your own business." Andrea stomped off. She had to fight to hold back tears, to hold back memories. No, Winn didn't need to know she could defend herself. Nobody needed to know. The element of surprise served in her favor. Besides, she wasn't going to go out with Winn. Maybe nobody, ever again.

***

Winn kept his eyes on the road, but all he saw was that beautiful, angelic face. Andrea worked right alongside the men, but the depth of her dark blue eyes exposed vulnerability, sensitivity, and something else. Fear? Why would she be afraid of anything? She was perfect—smart, strong, beautiful, loved. She might be a sweet, innocent sheep, but the men in her family were sheepdogs—they would fight to the death to protect her. Anybody could see that. Only an idiot would invade that safety shield.

It was different with Janae. Her prideful, overprotective family tried to control her and everyone who came in contact with her.

The female vocalist on the radio twanged about a hard-hearted man breaking her heart, so he punched the knob to turn it off. He never did anything to hurt Janae, but the Fontaines let him know from the beginning that he wasn't good enough for their precious, high-bred daughter. He wondered sometimes if Janae picked him just to spite them, to show them they couldn't completely control her.

After the accident, they tried to take Charity because they could give her everything, and he could give her nothing. But they were wrong. He could love her and make her feel loved. He would never treat his daughter like a trophy. She wouldn't have to dress or act a certain way. Charity wouldn't have to share in their society charade.

When he walked in the house, he dangled the cookies in the air. "Who wants a snickerdoodle?"

Charity jumped up to grab the bag. "I do!"

His mother frowned. "She already had dessert. Pudding. After *our* dinner."

"I don't think one cookie and a cup of milk will hurt her." He picked up his daughter and carried her to the kitchen.

"These are yummy," Charity said.

"They are. My friend's mom is a good cook."

She batted her eyelashes. "What's your friend's name?"

"The lady who baked the cookies is named Carmella."

Charity laughed. "Like the candy?"

Winn smiled. "Kind of like caramel. Finish your cookie so we can give you a bath and put you to bed."

"And then you'll read to me?"

"You've got it."

* * *

After Charity fell asleep, Winn's mother waited for him on the sofa, her arms crossed. "I think you should come home and spend some time with your daughter, especially after the long hours you've been putting in."

"I was helping some friends clean up after the tornado. You taught me to help others when I can, and a lot of people need help right now."

"Chari doesn't have a mother, so she needs her father to be a father."

Winn bit his tongue and counted to ten under his breath. "I am more of a father to her than my dad ever was. I'm home with her every night and every weekend. I'm not off riding the rodeo."

"You would be if you could."

"You didn't want me to follow in my dad's footsteps. You should be happy I gave up my dream." He didn't want to argue with his mother. He appreciated her help with Charity. He wanted her to have a better life now than she had with his dad, but there was only so much he could do.

"You're not the only one who had to give up dreams." She started toward her bedroom.

The victim mentality. "What are your dreams, Mom? What can I do to help you achieve them? Do you want me and Charity to leave, to move out?"

"No, I love having Chari here." She wiped tears from her eyes, her ultimate weapon to send him on a guilt trip. "If you moved out, the Fontaines would go back to court to get custody. And they might win this time."

***

Winn took a long hot shower. The steam around him couldn't compare to what boiled inside. As a kid, he tried to protect his mother from his father. She couldn't control her husband—she took whatever he dished out. How could someone so needy be so domineering? It was like she was trying to mold Winn into the man his dad failed to be. Life could be disappointing, but you grin and bear it, make the most of the hand you're dealt, and try to play your cards the best you can.

Chapter Five

"Thanks for dinner. The chicken cordon bleu, green bean almondine, and cheesecake were delicious," Andrea said as she began washing the pots and pans.

"I'm glad you could finally come for dinner." Katie wiped down the ice-gray, quartz countertop.

Everything in the white and red kitchen sparkled. Working together, Katie and Brooks had transformed this old house into a stylish home built on a foundation of love. Andrea wondered if she would ever have anything like it.

As if reading her thoughts, Katie asked, "Have you seen Winn lately?"

Andrea shook her head. "He stopped by once while we were cleaning up."

"He seemed nice. Cute, too." Katie hung up the dish towel. "So what happened?"

"Nothing happened." Andrea emptied the dishwater, rinsed, and dried her hands. "We met in a tornado. I invited him to the house for dinner to thank him for helping me keep calm until we were rescued. That's it. End of story."

Katie nodded. "Would you like a cappuccino—decaf? I can't

drink caffeine until after the baby is born." She started the machine and set two bright red mugs on the bar. After pouring the drinks she sat on the stool next to her sister-in-law. "We've never talked about your love life. Was there a special guy when you were in vet school?"

Andrea stared into her cup of cappuccino. "I was too busy studying to have much of a social life."

Katie raised her eyebrows. "What about college? Did you date then?"

Andrea felt the blush creep up her neck. The knot in her stomach tightened. "Not much." She sipped her drink. "Not many people end up marrying their childhood sweetheart."

"You didn't date much in high school, either. You were pretty picky." She grinned. "Brooks and I are truly blessed. The years we were apart made me realize how very special he is and how much I love him." Her diamond glittered as she patted Andrea's hand. "I pray that someday you will find a man to love, someone who loves you like Brooks loves me."

"There aren't many men like Brooks, but don't tell him I said so. I don't want him to get the big head." She traced the rim of the mug with her index finger. "How are you feeling? I've heard the last trimester is the hardest."

"I feel great, but I do get tired." Katie rubbed her baby bump. "Brooks is great to help with Austin now that school's out. It's hard for him to have time to write with his little shadow on his heels." She sipped her drink. "I make Austin lie down after lunch and read. That gives Brooks some solitude in addition to the early morning hours."

"Does he share his songs with you as he's writing?"

"Only if he's having trouble with a line coming together." She paused. "I feel honored to be the first person to hear each new song. Sometimes he has to make changes to suit a particular singer since Canada Jones isn't the only artist he writes for."

Andrea nodded. It must be nice to feel honored by a man. Looking around the kitchen, she asked, "Could you help me decorate my bedroom and bathroom at the clinic? I love the southwest décor you have in your master bed and bath. I'm going with rustic western for the reception area. Abuelo made a horseshoe hat rack and magazine stand. I'll add a few pictures of animals, and the lobby will be done. But since I'm going to live there, I'd like my bedroom and bath to be more personal and homey."

Katie's eyes danced. "I'd love to. Let me get my laptop."

Andrea found red and turquoise bedding similar to what Brooks and Katie had. At the shopping cart check out, Katie inserted her credit card information, insisting that she and Brooks wanted to give Andrea the items as a house-warming gift.

"I can't let you do that. I'm not a charity case."

Katie looked offended. "Who said anything about charity? We're family. Let us be blessed by giving you a gift."

***

On the drive back to her parents' home, Andrea thought about Winn. He did seem like an okay guy, down to earth, and hard working. He acted respectful and thoughtful of his mother, but appearances could be deceiving. Katie was right—he was cute, more than cute, but looks weren't the same as character. Could she trust him or any man ever again?

Brooks was special. Blinded by fame and fortune, even he lost his way for a while. *God, thank You for bringing Brooks and Katie home and back together. I pray they will live their happily ever after. When I think of the old Sonny James song, I wonder if there is just one love for everyone? I haven't found mine. Pretty soon I'll be too old for "Young Love"—that's okay because I'm definitely not ready to try dating again. I am picky, and I don't want to settle.*

***

The next week, Winn walked into the vet clinic as the men were hanging sheetrock. "It looks like you guys are making great progress."

An unbidden smile slid across Andrea's face. "I'm hoping I can open up for business soon."

Winn nodded. "I'm not a carpenter, but I can swing a hammer."

"Let me give you the grand tour." Waving her arm she said, "This of course is the lobby/reception area." He followed her through the two by four frames. "These two rooms will be the exam rooms. This is the operating room." She opened a door in the center of the building. "This is the best part—the safe room and supply closet. Step inside." When he obeyed, she closed the door. "See how much more comfortable this is than the little closet we were in during the tornado?"

He flashed his smile and his eyes twinkled. "I'm just glad you shared that little closet with me. Otherwise, I might not be standing here today."

She felt the blush heat up her face. "I'm glad you were here. Otherwise I might have died from fright."

"No, you're tougher than that. You're a survivor." His face looked sincere, but he didn't know her, didn't know what she'd been through.

She felt that familiar knot in her stomach. Yes, she survived, but the emotional scars remained. She opened the door. "My bedroom and bathroom will be back there. It won't be finished for a few weeks, but there's no hurry for that." Returning to the lobby she said, "I'm going to leave the bare concrete floor, at least for now. The cowboy church has a concrete floor. If it's good enough for church, it's good enough for my vet clinic." She handed him a hammer. "You can hammer while I take a break."

Winn took off his Co-op shirt. Andrea watched his muscles flex beneath his t-shirt as he swung the hammer. He didn't look like a bodybuilder, but he looked good, really good. *What is wrong with you?* She shook her head and reached for the hammer. "Okay, I'm rested enough to get back to work."

"Trying to get rid of me so soon?" He put the hammer behind his back.

"No, I just don't want to take advantage of you." She reached for the hammer, but jerked away when her arm brushed his. The manly scent of his sweat made her lightheaded.

He laughed. "You can't take advantage of someone who doesn't want to be taken advantage of."

She recoiled. *That doesn't stop some people from trying.*

He handed her the hammer. "I'll get the next piece of sheetrock and hold it in place while you hammer."

Andrea took a few deep breaths and mentally counted to ten. With his arms and legs spread across the sheetrock, she hammered, careful not to touch him.

Thirty minutes later, her mother walked in the door. "Winn, it's nice to see you." Setting the picnic basket on the floor, she said, "I hope you can stay and eat with us. I made brisket sandwiches, and some snickerdoodles."

He looked at his watch. "Thanks, but I better head on home. I have some chores to do before dark."

"You can take something with you."

"Thank you, Mrs. Travis, but my mother will have dinner ready."

Carmella pulled out a plastic bag of cookies. "Would you like some cookies?"

"Maybe just a couple. Your cookies are delicious."

After he left, the family sat in lawn chairs outside. Carmella said grace and Abuelo made the sign of the cross. Even though her father had come a long way, he still wouldn't pray out loud. She'd never heard either of her grandfathers pray, but Abuelo talked about God's goodness and love. At least they were all attending the cowboy church, to hear Brooks sing if for no other reason.

Looking up from her musing, all eyes were on Andrea. She took a drink of her water and continued eating.

Finally her mother broke the silence. "Winn seems like a nice young man."

Gramps stretched out his long legs. "He better be nice or Andrea will whoop up on him."

"Nieta is a lady."Abuela grinned at his granddaughter. "And if Winn is smart, he'll be a gentleman."

Smart has nothing to do with it. "Don't get any ideas. He may be a nice guy, but that's it." Andrea threw her water bottle in the trash and walked inside.

"Famous last words," Dustin said. "Who wants to bet we'll be planning another wedding within the year?"

Gramps shook his head and stuffed his lip with dip.

"You may be right." Abuelo showed his sage smile. "I bet within six months."

***

"Are these cookies from the candy lady?" Charity smiled as she reached for the bag.

"Yes, but you can't have one until after you eat your dinner." Winn kissed his daughter's blond head.

55

His mother raised her eyebrows. "The candy lady?"

"My friend's mother is named Carmella."

"Who is your friend?"

"Just a friend, Mom, nothing more."

After putting Charity to bed, Winn lay awake thinking about Andrea. Could they be friends, just friends? He had known girls in high school who were just friends, but then he was too shy to make a move. In college, with a little help from Budweiser and Jim Beam, he became a party animal. That's how he met Janae. She was wild enough to be exciting without being disgusting. When she found out she was pregnant, she quit drinking. He didn't know she had started again until after the accident. Between school, a part-time job, and rodeo on the weekends, he wasn't around enough to know what she was doing. Then it was too late.

To keep his daughter, he had to get his life together. He quit school and came home so his mom could help take care of the baby. He vowed he would never drink again. He didn't want Charity to become an orphan or grow up with a dad like his. He was lucky they were hiring at the co-op, and his mom helped him get the job. It wasn't his original dream, but it provided a good, honest living, and he enjoyed working with a great team of guys.

Chapter Six

Winn stopped by the clinic every day after work to help with the sheet rock, the tape and bedding, the plaster, and painting. "Tomorrow's the big day we move everything in. Monday I'll be open for business." Andrea's smile lit up her face.

Winn could look at that face forever. He melted beneath the warmth of her smile. His hands felt clammy. To help him chill, he took a long drink of cold water.

"Winn, could you come to church with us Sunday? Katie and Brooks are having a cookout afterwards to help celebrate my reopening." Andrea looked at him with those deep blue eyes, and he felt himself sinking.

He walked to the trash can to distance himself from her. "My mom likes to do a big dinner thing on Sundays. It's important to her." He finished his bottle of water and threw it away. "What if I take you to dinner Saturday night? I would like to pay back your hospitality."

"You don't need to pay back anything. I feel indebted to you for all the work you've done around here."

He took a deep breath. "I'd like to take you out to dinner. Just you and me."

"If I go to dinner with you on Saturday, will you go to church

57

with me on Sunday?"

He didn't like being pressured. Janae's parents had pressured him to go to their church. The whole thing made him uncomfortable: the crystal chandeliers, the huge pipe organ and grand piano, the stained glass windows, the stuffy suits and designer dresses, the preacher who turned God into a three-syllable word. His throat constricted just thinking about it.

"Do you go to church?" Andrea asked, her gentle voice expressing sincerity.

He shook his head. "Is that a requirement before we can be friends?"

She looked wounded. "I thought we were already friends."

Friends? Can we be just friends? "Friends spend time together. We've worked together. I'd like to have some fun—time to relax, talk, laugh, get to know each other better." He moved closer to her.

She stepped back, crossed her arms protectively across her stomach, and looked at the ground. "Just to let you know, I don't drink, and I don't like to be around people who do. I don't go to clubs."

Wow! Where did that come from? He shook his head. "I don't drink or go to clubs, either, just to let you know." He smiled and gestured with his hands. "But I do eat. You eat. Maybe we could eat together. Sometime, somewhere, at a restaurant."

She nodded, avoiding his eyes. "Um, maybe we could go to

Pat's?"

"I was thinking of something a little nicer, maybe in Lubbock. We could go to a movie, if you want."

"I'm not sure what time we'll get everything moved in tomorrow. How about next Saturday?"

Winn felt his heart inflate. He worked to control his voice. The last thing he wanted was to sound like a pubescent boy. "Sounds great. I'll call you sometime this week." As he walked to his pickup, he hoped he wasn't prancing. He could feel the ground shake beneath his feet. He turned to wave before driving away. She smiled and gave a little Miss America wave. On the highway, he pumped his fist in the air. *Yes, finally!*

***

That night, Andrea struggled to sleep. *Lord, Winn does seem like an okay guy, well, more than okay. He's hard working. He makes me laugh. He seems kind and thoughtful. He is pleasing to the eye, but so was the apple, or whatever the forbidden fruit was. Katie's right, I've always been picky, but then when I did pick, it was a rotten choice. I can't trust myself, and I don't know if I can trust Winn. I don't think he's a Christian, or at least not a practicing one. That is important to me.*

She turned on her phone and searched the internet for Bible verses about trust. Switching on the bedside lamp, she opened the nightstand drawer and wrote the following verses on colored index cards:

Psalm 37:5 "Commit thy way unto the LORD; trust also in him; and he shall bring it to pass."

Psalm 56:3-4 "What time I am afraid, I will trust in thee. In God I will praise his word, in God I have put my trust; I will not fear what flesh can do unto me."

Proverbs 3:5 "Trust in the LORD with all thine heart; and lean not unto thine own understanding."

Ephesians 6:10 "Finally, be strong in the Lord and in his mighty power."

Okay, Lord, I don't want to be afraid any longer. I want to trust You. I am weak, but You are strong.

With the words of "Jesus Loves Me" playing in her mind, she fell into a restful sleep, wrapped in the arms of God.

The next morning, she read her index cards several times. She sang "Jesus Loves Me" while taking her shower. *Thank You, Lord for loving me, always and forever. This is the day You have made. I will rejoice and be glad in it. I'm trusting You to show me Your way. When I am afraid, I will stop and praise You. I'm depending on You for strength. I can do all things with Your help.*

Before breakfast, Andrea wrote the trust verses on a sheet of paper, folded it, and put it in her jeans pocket. Throughout the week, she read the verses morning and evening. If negative thoughts crept into her mind, she patted her pocket and whispered a prayer of thanksgiving for God's promises.

Wednesday at 8:45 pm, Andrea's phone rang. Winn. Her pulse quickened, and she patted the index cards on her nightstand before answering. Taking a deep breath, she finally said, "Hi, Winn."

"I hope it's not too late to call. You aren't in bed are you?"

She got out of bed and walked to her desk. "No, I was just reading."

"You reading anything good?"

"Yes, the greatest book ever written."

"The greatest book ever written? Let me guess, is it *The Man Who Rode Midnight* by Elmer Kelton?"

She rolled her shoulders. "No, but I have read that, and it is a great book."

"Okay, are you reading one of the *Hank the Cowdog* books?"

She giggled. "No, I haven't read those for years. What is your favorite *Hank the Cowdog* book?"

"*Moonlight Madness.* Have you ever listened to the audio version?"

"No, I just read them when I was in grade school."

"John R. Erickson does all the voices and sings the songs. This is my favorite from *Moonlight Madness.*" He took a deep breath and began singing a song about watermelon, cantaloupe, and black-eyed peas.

Andrea laughed until her sides hurt.

"You don't like my singing?"

"Oh, I love it." She laughed again.

"Well, I have to admit I can't sing like your family, but I do love that song."

She wanted to control her laughter, but it felt so good. Laughter is good for the soul, and her soul needed it. "I can't sing, either, so we'd make a good pair."

Silence. "I think we would make a good pair," he whispered.

Oh, my why did she say that? How should she respond?

"So, what is your favorite Hank book?"

She tried to steady her voice. "Um, I haven't thought about them for years." She lay down on her bed, closed her eyes, jiggled her foot, and said, "Something about Madame Moonshine and a snake when Hank's eyes get crossed. Do you remember that one?"

He laughed. "Yes, the witchy witch. That is funny." He took a breath. "Okay, I give up. What book were you reading?"

"The greatest book ever written is the Bible. If you read the Bible, what is your favorite passage?"

"I like David and Goliath, the little guy beating the big strong guy." Pausing, his voice a husky whisper. "In case you haven't noticed, I'm not very big."

"I have noticed." *Yes, I've noticed how you look.* "I mean, there's nothing wrong with the way you look, or your size." She stretched and flexed her feet, wiggled her toes, relaxing movements.

"All the men in your family are tall."

"So what? That doesn't matter to me." She toyed with a lock of hair. "You're taller than me."

He asked, "What does matter to you?"

"Character. Honesty. Integrity. Loyalty. Work ethic. Thoughtfulness. Consideration. Humility. Patience. Kindness. Goodness. Faithfulness. Gentleness. Self-control." *Yes, Lord, self-control is so important.*

"You rattled off that long list pretty fast."

She hugged herself. "I have a list. I made it in high school, and I have it memorized."

"Pretty tough list." He whistled. "Which is most important?"

"They're all important. Honesty is non-negotiable. Without honesty, nothing else matters."

"Well, I work hard. I try to be good and honest and thoughtful. I've always been loyal and faithful to my friends." He paused. "I don't know how gentle I am, more like a bull in a China closet."

"Are you gentle with people and animals? That's more important than stuff."

"Sometimes you have to be firm with animals, but never cruel. I'm good with kids, and I always treat a lady like a lady."

"Really?"

"Yes, like Robin Hood, my hero—the underdog winning against all odds." He exhaled. "The cowboy way is a lot like the code of chivalry."

"Sounds heroic, like a knight in shining armor."

"Well, cowboys and knights fight for what's right. Knights valued honesty, honor, and glory. True cowboys do, too. Knights respected and honored ladies, same with cowboys. Knighthood was a brotherhood. Cowboys have a special bond—so do linemen. I guess linemen are like knights. We travel the countryside risking our lives to provide power for people. We have each other's back."

"I never read much about knights, but I think what you do is very noble."

"Didn't you read *Sir Gawain and the Green Knight*? It was the best thing I read in college."

"I didn't know you went to college. Where did you go?"

"I went to Tech for a couple of years." He let out a harsh breath. "I only went because I had a rodeo scholarship. School wasn't my thing."

"It sounds like you enjoy reading. What was your area of study?"

"Ag and animal science."

"Do you think you'll ever go back to school?"

"Maybe someday I'll have the desire to go back, but not now. I enjoy what I do." He paused and Andrea wondered if he regretted his decision. "I read a lot about genetics and animal breeding because I'd like to improve my cattle stock before I try to increase my herd."

They talked about different cattle breeds, leading breeders, artificial insemination. After saying goodbye, Andrea couldn't believe how late it was. She had never talked that long on the phone to anyone except Katie, a long time ago, when they were kids, before time changed everything. The past year their relationship had moved from cold to cordial to friendly. Andrea wished they could regain the intimacy they once shared. Once upon a time, she felt closer to Katie than she did her own sister. She wished she could talk to Katie about Winn, about her secret dreams and disappointments, about what happened in vet school. She couldn't talk to Celina about those things. It felt comfortable talking to Winn, safe. But would she feel safe Saturday night, alone with him in a car, on the desolate road to Lubbock?

She opened her Bible and continued reading in Ephesians Chapter Six. She searched the internet and found a picture of a Christian knight wearing the full armor of God. *Tomorrow I'll print this and put it in my Bible as a visual of what I need to do every day so I can be strong in You, Lord.*

She opened her folded paper with her trust verses. On the backside, she wrote: "Put on the full armor of God so you can take your stand against the devil's schemes." Then she listed each piece of armor. She turned out her light and prayed. *Dear Lord, please help me to draw on Your mighty power so I can be strong.*

When sleep finally came, she dreamed of Winn, riding a white steed, wearing shiny armor, carrying a Crusader's shield, wielding a two-edged sword. She saw herself in a dark forest, tangled tree limbs blocking her path. She felt helpless, lost, and alone. Winn challenged the dark knight, knocked his sword out of his hand and chased him away. He cleared a path through the trees, cutting the limbs, letting the light shine around her. He picked her up and put her on his horse, leading her from the darkness. She felt like Sleeping Beauty, being awakened to a new life of promise and possibilities.

Chapter Seven

Winn found his Children's Bible Story book in his closet and began reading it to Chari at bedtime, starting with David and Goliath, Jonah and the whale. He read the creation account in Genesis, Baby Moses in the bulrushes, and Baby Jesus in the manger. He remembered going to Vacation Bible School when he was a kid. His mother took him to Sunday School sometimes when his dad was riding the rodeo circuit. He went to a few youth activities in junior high, but he was too shy to feel really comfortable. After his dad died, he never went to church, until he met Janae. Her family's church in Dallas was way out of his comfort zone. He can still remember the hissy fit her parents threw when they found out he and Janae were married by the justice of the peace. They wanted a big showy wedding, but Janae put her foot down and said she was tired of playing their puppet. Just another thing they held against him.

He wondered about the cowboy church Andrea talked about. He might feel comfortable around other cowboys. But he wasn't ready to chance it yet—one thing at a time. After they got to know each other better, if she still liked him, he would tell her about Charity. No matter how much he liked Andrea, he couldn't take a chance on hurting his little girl. He couldn't let her get attached to someone just to be disappointed.

***

Saturday after finishing his ranch work, he washed and polished his pickup. Gleaming in the sunlight, it made him think of Andrea's remark about a knight in shining armor. He was just an ordinary guy, a common man, but he was honest and honorable. Well, he tried. Keeping Charity a secret wasn't being dishonest, because he needed to be cautious and protective. He was his little girl's knight. Andrea didn't need a knight. She was strong, independent, smart, and beautiful. Her dad, grandfathers, and brother were her protectors. She was perfect and had a perfect life. But sometimes a person needed more than family. He loved Charity and his mother, but there was something missing, an emptiness in his heart. He wondered if Andrea would have room in her life for a man, someone ordinary like him, and room for Charity.

He didn't have a helmet or armor, but he wore his new white Stetson, a white starched George Strait shirt, and Wranglers. He spit shined his black Justin boots and wore his prize buckle and his dress belt. Looking in the full-length mirror, he said, "This is the best I can do. I hope it's good enough."

When he kissed Charity, she said, "You look pretty."

He laughed. "Girls look pretty. Men look handsome."

She giggled. "You look han-some, and you smell good, too."

"I'm wearing the aftershave you gave me for my birthday." He

68

twirled her around and set her on the sofa next to her grandmother. "Don't forget to say your prayers before you go to sleep."

"You won't be home to read a Bible story to me?" She pooched out her lip.

"Not tonight, but I bet your Gamma will, won't you Mom?"

Faith hugged her granddaughter. "Yes, I'll read to you after your bath." She raised her eyebrows. "A special date?"

"Just a friend." He hugged his mother.

She twisted her lip between a frown and a smirk. Nodding her head, she said, "Be careful and be good."

"Always."

***

On the drive to the T-C Quarter Horse Ranch, Winn kept telling himself to be calm. Andrea was *just* a friend. She could be more, maybe, but right now she was just a friend. As soon as he saw her, he knew he wanted so much more. The purple sundress made her dark blue eyes look almost purple. The skirt swished around her shapely legs, the best ones he'd ever seen, and being a leg man, he'd looked at a lot of legs.

He felt the scrutiny of the male members of her family. The only one missing was her brother Brooks. Her mother smiled, the same pleasant smile Andrea had. She told them to stay safe and have fun, the mother thing. Her father didn't say anything. He didn't have to. His steely stare stated a warning—be good to my daughter, or else. Clearly the boss of the bunch, Dean Travis, her Gramps, reminded

Winn of the Duke, the strong silent type. Roberto Cordova, her Abuelo, grinned like a boy bursting to tell a secret.

When he opened the pickup door for her, Winn said, "You smell really sweet."

"Thanks, you do, too." She smiled. "Not sweet. You smell nice…manly."

He laughed. "Good because I don't want to be a girly man." She blushed.

On the drive to Lubbock, Winn told Andrea about some of his latest adventures as a lineman. Her laughter helped him relax. He asked about the clinic and listened attentively.

***

At Las Brisas Restaurant, Winn told the greeter they had reservations on the patio. Andrea took in the white table cloths, red napkins, and wine glasses. Their table sat across from the waterfall. The bubbling water blended with the cooing of birds creating a relaxing atmosphere. The fountain spray sent ripples throughout the pond creating flutters up her spine. The band in the background played soothing, romantic music.

When the waiter brought the menus, Winn asked him to take away the wine glasses and bring them water. Andrea smiled and nodded her thanks. Looking at the menu, she felt the smile slide off her face. She closed it and whispered, "We can just order an appetizer and go somewhere else for dinner."

He leaned forward and whispered, "Why would we do that?"

70

"Because it's so expensive."

"I want our first dinner to be memorable." He winked. "Order whatever you want. You're worth it."

She looked at the choices. Without looking at him, she asked, "What would you recommend?"

"I'm going to order the prime rib with Au jus and creamed horseradish, baked potato, Caesar salad, and sautéed asparagus."

She nodded. "Have you ever tried the Filet Mignon rolled in raspberry Chipotle Sauce, encrusted in pecans, and topped with a Jalapeno Cream Cheese?"

"I haven't, but I've heard it's good."

"Okay, only I'll order that with the asparagus, truffle mashed potatoes, and a house salad."

They talked freely during dinner. She loved Winn's quick wit and sense of humor. The atmosphere put her at ease. The steak was the best she had ever eaten, even though she would never pay that much for a meal. The waiter filled their water glasses and asked if they would like dessert. He suggested the Brandy Butter Apple Dumpling or the Tableside Bananas Foster for Two.

Andrea knew she didn't want anything with brandy, so she asked about the Bananas Foster. The waiter said, "It is vanilla bean ice cream and fresh bananas with a sauce made of butter, brown sugar, cinnamon, rum and banana liqueur that is flambéed at your table." She shook her head. "We also have carrot cake with warm cream cheese icing and New York cheesecake with fresh berry sauce."

"Winn, you can get dessert if you want, but, really, I can't eat another bite."

He nodded. "Thank you. We're ready for our ticket."

Walking to the pickup, Winn asked, "Would you like to go to the movies?"

"It's been a hectic couple of weeks, and I'm afraid I would fall asleep in the theater or on the drive back home. Then you'd have to carry me in."

He flexed his biceps. "I could do that."

She laughed. "Dead weight is pretty heavy."

"I handle heifers that weigh more than you."

She frowned. "Are you comparing me to a heifer?"

The blush crept up his neck and face, looking like he'd been branded. "I didn't mean it like that. I meant…"

She averted her gaze. "It's okay. I know what you meant." His red face formed a rich contrast to his brilliant white shirt. *I wonder if he knows how cute he is.*

Winn turned on his iPod and Glenn Campbell belted out the lyrics to "Wichita Lineman". He started the pickup and pulled onto the highway. "I downloaded this for you."

When "Galveston" began playing, Andrea broke the silence. "Abuelo won't sing that song because both he and Gramps were in Vietnam. The song brings back memories they won't talk about."

He picked up the iPod. "I can skip it."

"No, I like the song. I think our generation needs to remember what the Vietnam vets went through, giving up their youth, leaving home and family, then being treated like trash when they came home."

He nodded. "Yeah, my grandfather was killed in Vietnam, so my dad never knew his father. He didn't have a good relationship with his step-dad and left to follow the rodeo as soon as he was old enough."

"That's sad." They rode on in silence until "Rhinestone Cowboy" began playing. "Brooks said that's how he felt when he was chasing after the limelight. I'm glad he found himself and came back home."

"Yeah, it's the same with the rodeo." He waved his hands as they drove around Texas Tech. "Here's my old stomping grounds."

"I bet you were a player."

"Not me." His low, soft laugh was irresistible.

"All those rodeo queens and barrel racers, I bet they were all over you."

He stared at her. "Why would you say that?"

"Well, you are pretty cute, and funny, and rodeo girls like rodeo guys." *I might as well be honest.*

***

He focused on the road. "I was pretty shy and didn't date a lot."

"Hasn't there ever been a special girl?"

Tell her the truth. Tell her now. He shook his head. "There was one." His breath stopped, his voice trembled. What to say. "Let's just say my heart still hurts."

She looked out the side window. "I'm sorry."

Yeah me, too. He pulled into the parking lot at J & B Coffee House. "You ever been here?"

She shook her head. "I'm not much of a coffee drinker."

He opened his door and walked around to open hers. "They have tea, cookies, muffins, chocolate covered strawberries, and other stuff."

He ordered a big cup of coffee and two chocolate covered strawberries. She ordered a cherry limeade. They sat at a table on the patio and watched the traffic zoom past. "City people go too fast. They need to slow down and enjoy life." He sipped his coffee. "This is a perfect night. No clouds. Nice little breeze, not too windy."

"Yes, I love watching the stars, in the country, where it's quiet."

He handed her a strawberry. "Is it too loud for you? We can go anytime."

"No, no. Enjoy your big cup of coffee." She bit into the strawberry. "Umm, this is good."

He wrapped his hands around his mug. "I like a real cup of real coffee. I hate drinking that convenience store stuff out of those Styrofoam cups."

When they got back in the pickup, he asked, "Do you like

George Strait?"

"The greatest country singer of all time? But don't tell my family I said so."

"Who do they think is the greatest?"

She rolled her eyes. "Brooks Travis, of course. After him, they all have different favorites, all the old classic country singers."

They listened to "Amarillo by Morning" in silence. When "I Cross My Heart" came on, she said, "True love, everlasting love, what all the romance books and movies are about, what every woman dreams of."

He heard the sadness in her voice. Someone had broken her heart. He'd like to find the guy and break him in two. "True love does exist, between the right man and woman." *He hoped it could exist more than once.*

"Check Yes or No" played next. Andrea said, "That's Brooks and Katie's song. They fell in love in elementary school, but the cowboy rode away. I'm so glad they got back together. I pray they will live their happily ever after."

He nodded. His and Janae's happily ever after wasn't always happy, and it didn't last forever.

Canada Jones played next. "Did you know Brooks wrote that song? He wrote several of Canada's top hits."

"I didn't know that. I just like the songs."

She tucked her hair behind her ear. "Brooks says he's happy to stay at home, sing at the Cowboy Church, and write songs. He hated being on the road."

Winn parked in the driveway at the T-C Quarter Horse Ranch, turned on the dome light, pulled a gift bag from behind the seat, and handed it to her.

"Is this for me?"

He laughed. "Of course it's for you."

She removed the tissue paper and pulled out two CDs. "Hank the Cowdog?" She smiled. "Thank you."

"I thought you could listen to them while you're driving around."

"Thanks. I can't wait to hear the watermelon song."

He got out and walked around to open her door. When they reached the front porch, he said. "I had a good time tonight. I hope we can do this again, soon."

"Me, too." She said good night, opened the door, and stepped inside.

"Good night," he said and backed off the porch. At his pickup, he waved. She gave him a quick wave and closed the door.

Chapter Eight

The next week, Andrea listened to Her *Hank the Cowdog* CDs as she drove around making calls or when she was alone at the clinic. She thought of Winn, a lot. She liked him, liked everything about him—except that he didn't go to church. A person could be a Christian and not go to church, but as a little girl, when she saw pictures on church bulletins of a family walking into church together, holding hands, she knew that's what she wanted. Having an absent dad, she missed out on so much while growing up.

Thank You, Lord, for this past year, reconciling our family. My dad is trying to make up for lost time. I've always known he loved me, even if he couldn't say it, and I loved him. I'm grateful for Abuelo and Gramps, but sometimes I wanted my dad. And when I find a man, I want one who will be there for me and our kids, when we have them. That is my dream, Lord. You have promised to give us the desires of our heart if we trust in You. I'm not ready for a relationship yet, but I am asking You to heal my heart so, when the time is right, in Your time, I will be ready.

Wednesday evening Andrea toyed with the idea of calling Winn. At 8:30, she took the plunge. After five rings, she was just about to disconnect. Then he answered.

"Hey, this is Andrea."

He laughed. "I know—caller ID. How are you?"

"I'm good." She tucked her hair behind her ear. "I, um, I just wanted to call and thank you for the CDs. I enjoyed listening to them."

"I'm glad you liked them." She heard night noises and knew he was outside. "I listen to the CDs when I'm driving around making calls. It helps pass the time."

His voice sounded tense, and she wondered if she caught him at a bad time, if she should have called at all. "How has your week been?"

"Busy. I'm on call and was out last night till after midnight. Some kid ran into a pole and knocked the lines down."

"Oh, no! Was he hurt?"

"The ambulance was gone by the time I got there. He was hurt but not dead."

"Well, I'm sure you're tired, so I'll let you go."

"No, no. Don't go." His breath quickened. "Tell me about your week. Hopefully it's been better than mine."

She told him about delivering twin horses at her family's ranch. "It's rare for twin horses to be born and both survive. They are beautiful, just like their mother." She described the sire, his bloodline, and the roping competitions he's won. "Abuelo is a horse whisperer. The colt and filly already love him almost as much as their mama. Gramps will begin getting them used to a rope soon. I know they will be champions."

"It seems like you have the perfect family, everyone working together and all that."

She mused. "The perfect family does not exist." She sat crossed legged on the floor and inhaled deeply. "Abuelo, patient and wise, can get along with anyone. My mom, the nurturer, wants to take care of everyone. Gramps, the leader of the pack, works hard but can be controlling and demanding. My dad, the wanderer, competed in rodeo to help get the ranch established, but I think he became addicted to winning, collecting buckles and trophy saddles, making money."

"He was the best roper I've ever seen."

"Yes, but he was gone more than he was here." She stretched and took another deep breath. "It felt awkward when he came home for good, especially with Brooks. He's trying to mend fences, and things are getting better."

"It seems like you have a great relationship with him."

"Being the baby, I was always Daddy's girl. When he was around, I shadowed him, and he doted on me." She took another deep breath.

"What are you doing?"

"What do you mean?"

He laughed. "I can hear you breathing."

I'm glad he can't see my blush. "I'm doing my Yoga stretches and relaxation breathing."

"After a week like this, maybe I should try that."

"I could teach you, sometime, if you'd like."

He laughed again. "As long as the guys at work don't find out."

"I couldn't tell them because I don't know them."

"You met Keith the night of the tornado." He took a deep breath, and she wondered if he was mimicking her. "I'm on call through this weekend. Maybe we could go out to dinner next week."

"That sounds good." She giggled. "Since you have to eat, and I have to eat, maybe we could eat together, sometime." She took another deep breath. "The next weekend is the big Fourth of July celebration and street dance. Will you be there?"

Winn stiffened. *Is she asking me to the dance? What if someone saw us, someone who knows about Charity?*

"I wasn't asking you to go with me. I just asked if you were going." He heard the hurt in her voice, as if she could read his mind.

"I hadn't thought about going to the dance, but if I went, I would want to go with you."

"Maybe I'll see you then. Goodnight." She disconnected the call.

Did I just blow it? Talk about being between a rock and a hard place. He stomped out to the barn, stirring up dust with every step. What should he do? *Tell her about Charity.*

He turned on his phone and dialed Andrea's number. Five rings before she answered. "Andrea, would you go to the Fourth of July dance with me?"

He heard her take another deep breath. "No, but if you go, I'll see you there."

He shook his head. Did he misread what she said earlier? "Why won't you go with me?"

"Because." She took another deep breath. "It's a big thing for our family to go together." Another deep breath. "Brooks and the Cowboy Church band will be playing part of the time. When the country band from Lubbock plays, maybe we can dance . . . if we run into each other."

"I would like that." He sighed. "Take your phone in case we don't *just* run into each other."

"Okay." She took another deep breath. He hoped she was calm and relaxed instead of angry. "Are you going to the rodeo before the dance?"

What should he say? "I haven't been to a rodeo since I quit bull riding."

"Why did you quit?" she asked, her voice soft and low.

Tell her. He shook his head. "I came face-to-face with death, and decided I wanted to live." *I needed to live for my little girl.*

"So you became a lineman?"

"If I pay attention and respect electricity, I know I'm safe. I respect bulls, but they're unpredictable." He leaned against the barn, closed his eyes, and inhaled the sweet smell of hay. "My dad was like yours—gone more than he was home. I don't want that kind of life. I like being home in my own bed every night. I'm okay with being an ordinary guy, doing an honest day's labor, working with good ole boys."

"I think that's honorable."

"I make a decent living, but I'll never be rich."

"Money's not everything." He heard the disappointment in her voice. "After rebuilding the clinic, I won't even make a decent living for a while." She sighed. "On the bright side, my bedroom and bathroom at the clinic should be finished this weekend. Then I'll at least have my own place. It will be better than living in my dad's living quarters' horse trailer, roomier, and more comfortable."

"That's good. If I get off work at a decent time, maybe I can stop by and help sometime this week."

"The space is pretty tight. I'm not sure there would be room for you."

There may not room for me in her life, either. "Well. I'll drop by to see you sometime this week if I get a chance."

"I'd like that."

"Good night, Andrea."

"Good night, Winn."

***

Winn didn't drop by to see Andrea all week. She stayed busy during the day with her practice and at night finishing her bedroom and bath. Saturday, she moved in. The bedding and bath linens Brooks and Katie bought her arrived, along with curtains Katie ordered later—for a surprise. She brought the twin bed, night stand,

and dresser from the bedroom she had shared with her older sister Celina. Her mother said they needed to buy a queen-size bed for guests. They never had overnight guests, but Celina and her husband would be home from Germany in the spring. Her parents offered to buy her new bedroom furniture, but Andrea already felt like she owed them a debt she could never repay.

Sunday evening after spending the day with her family, she stretched out on her bed and stared at the ceiling. The clinic was empty, no animals, no people. The sound of silence made her feel isolated. While in vet school, she lived in an apartment, but school, work, and studying kept her mind occupied, her body tired. Now her thoughts raced, reliving the day—church, dinner, laughter, the family singing on the porch, riding a powerful horse through the pasture with her dad. Images of Brooks and Katie flashed in her mind. The love they shared showed in their eyes, their smiles, their touches, especially when Brooks stroked her swollen stomach. And Austin. *Lord, I love that little boy.*

Andrea thought about Winn and wondered about his family. His dad was dead, and he lived with his mother, but she wondered if he had any extended family, cousins, nieces and nephews. She wondered if he liked kids. Watching Katie's pregnancy progress stimulated Andrea's maternal instincts. She would love to have a husband and children someday, if she ever found someone she could trust and respect, someone who would love, honor, and cherish her.

When sleep finally overtook her, she dreamed of Winn

carrying a little boy with light brown hair and gray eyes, her holding hands with a little black-haired, blue-eyed girl, walking into church, not the picture imprinted on her memory of a big church with white columns and stained glass, but a cowboy church with country gospel playing in the background.

***

On Tuesday, Andrea's phone buzzed in her pocket as she rubbed her hands along the forelock of an Overa paint mare. Ignoring her phone, she told the owner, "She has navicular disease, but since we caught it early, it is treatable." Andrea drained the pus and gave the horse an injection of antibiotic. "Apply this paste every morning, and give her Bute once a day. I suggest you change farriers. Hank can put wedge horseshoes on her, which will alleviate the pressure and pain. Here's his card."

When she got into her pickup, she checked her phone. Winn. But he didn't leave a message. She pushed redial, but she got his voicemail. She disconnected. At 4:30 her phone rang. Caller ID showed Winn Timberman. She let it ring four times before taking a deep breath and answering. "Hey."

"Hey. I just saw that I missed a call from you."

"Uh-huh. I called because I missed a call from you." She relaxed hearing his teasing, playful laugh. "I was working on a horse when you called."

"And I was tied up, hanging on a pole when you called back."

She closed her eyes and remembered the first time she saw

him hanging on a pole, tossed to and fro before the tornado. "I'm glad the weather was calm, no wind today."

"A little breeze would have been nice. It got pretty hot." He took a deep breath. "I was in the area, so I called to see if I could bring you some lunch."

She thought of the yogurt and salad she had planned to eat. "I haven't had dinner yet."

"I can't come now. I got hot today." He laughed again. "Not the kind of hot you would like, sweaty hot."

"I'm used to sweaty men—the men in my family I mean." She sat down in the lobby. "I haven't showered yet, either. Since you have to eat, and I have to eat, maybe we could eat together, later, in an hour or so."

***

He thought about it. He would like to spend some time with her, but his mother probably had dinner ready. "I can't tonight. I never know for sure, but Thursday I may be in your area. Maybe we can eat lunch together then. If you're at the clinic, I could bring you something from Dairy Queen."

"I never know for sure where I'll be either, but Dairy Queen sounds good."

***

Thursday Winn didn't call Andrea until 4:00. "I got tied up at noon. I'm on my way back to the office, and I'll drive right by Dairy Queen. Can I get you something?"

85

"I ate yogurt and vegetable sticks for lunch, so maybe I can indulge in a Blizzard."

"I missed lunch, so I'm going to get a Flamethrower Grill Burger. You sure you don't want anything to eat?"

Her heart warmed at the thought of his hamburger, or was that sympathy indigestion "No, thank you. I'm eating with my family, but I would like a Chocolate Xtreme Blizzard."

"Okay. I'll see you in 15 to 20 minutes."

***

He walked in the clinic carrying a cardboard drink tray. "I cranked the AC way down to keep them cold. I hope they're not melted."

Andrea laughed. "I like it better a little melted, so I can slurp it." She put a straw in her cup and sipped. "Whoa, brain freeze."

"I think my brain melted today. Maybe this will cool me down." He held up a large Blizzard cup.

"Where's your hamburger?"

"I was starved, so I ate it on the way." He scooped chunks out of his cup.

"What do you have?"

"Banana Split Blizzard. Meat and cheese, bread and fries, lettuce and tomato, ice cream and fruit make it a well-balanced meal—right?"

She laughed. "Whatever you say." She dipped her spoon in her cup. "So how has your week been?"

"Hot and long. Nothing exciting. What about your week?"

"Slow. I was hoping you'd have some funny stories to tell me."

"Being a lineman isn't all excitement and adventure. Sometimes it's just grunge work." He winked. "But I do get to see some pretty sights." He took out his phone and showed her a picture. "Look at this sunrise."

"I love all the pinks and purples. With the windmill in the foreground, it looks like a calendar picture."

"This is the best view on our property." He took the phone back and clicked on another photo. "This is our newest baby bull."

"Oh, he is adorable." Andrea pushed a stray hair behind her ear. "Austin, Brooks and Katie's son, has a bull his other grandfather gave him. It's named Mighty Fine." She handed him back his phone "What are you going to name your bull?"

"Thunder Alley. He was born in the thunderstorm after the tornado."

"These are very good. Have you ever taken a photography course?"

"Actually I did take a couple classes in college." He put his phone in his pocket. "I have some better pictures taken with a real camera."

"I'd like to see them sometime."

"Sounds like a date . . . I mean a deal." His best pictures are of Charity, but he couldn't show those to Andrea, not yet. And pictures of Janae throughout her pregnancy and as a new mother, and Andrea would probably never want to see those.

She slurped the rest of her Blizzard through her straw and giggled. *God, I love her laughter, the way her eyes dance when she smiles. Reality check. I better go before my pickup turns into a pumpkin and my mother banishes me to the barn.*

He took his phone out and snapped a picture of her. "Now I have something really pretty to look at." She blushed, which made her even more alluring. "My mom probably has dinner ready, so I better go." *Yeah, I need to get away so I can catch my breath and clear my head.*

"Will you be able to eat so soon after eating that Flamethrower Burger?"

"I told you I was starved. That just stopped the gnawing in my stomach. I have room to eat enough to please my mom."

"That's nice that you are so thoughtful of your mother."

"I'm grateful for all she does." *Especially for Charity.*

"So maybe I'll see you Saturday?"

"I have some work to catch up on, so I won't make it to the rodeo. I'll try to see you at the dance."

"I'll be there, around, somewhere."

Her smile turned him into melted butter. He wanted to pull her into his arms and kiss her, but he knew he couldn't. It might be risky going to the dance, but he was willing to take a chance. He wanted to hold her close, to dance with her. If things went well, he would tell her about Charity.

***

After Winn drove away, alarm skittered through Andrea's stomach. What had she done? Was she ready to get that close to a man? To dance with him? But other people would be around. Her family would be close by if she needed them. She would make sure they were nearby before she agreed to dance with him, or anyone else.

God, I like Winn. I like him a lot. I'm just not sure I'm ready to trust him. Lord, all things are possible with you. Please help my unbelief.

Chapter Nine

Andrea enjoyed spending the day with her family, especially Austin. He competed in the junior roping contest and won first place. Brooks put the prize buckle on his belt, and the boy showed it to everyone. Dustin Travis beamed, showing off his grandson to all his fans. "Watch out, world. He's going to be better than I ever was."

"That'll be something since you were the best," the rodeo announcer said.

The family had set up a booth under an awning with a banner advertising the T-C Quarter Horse Ranch. They had brochures about their roping clinics, breeding stock, training programs, and horses available for sale. They also had brochures about the Kane Cattle Ranch, Katie's family ranch, and Andrea's veterinarian clinic. They took turns manning the booth, but everyone met to eat brisket sandwiches before the street dance started.

Richard Kane said, "We'll stay at the booth since we don't dance anyway."

Katie raised her eyebrows. "Umm, you danced at my wedding."

"That was your special day." Donna Kane blushed down to her Baptist roots. "This is totally different."

"Okay, but you don't know what you're missing." Katie took her husband's hand and led him into the swarm of dancers.

Abuelo asked Andrea if she would honor him with the first dance. Tall and graceful, he held her like a porcelain doll. Gramps stepped in for the next dance, a lively number where he spun her around like a top. Then she danced a slow dance with her dad and thought about the traditional father daughter dance at her wedding . . . someday. Brooks asked Andrea if she would dance with him while Katie took a break. Before the first stanza of "Waltz Across Texas" finished, Winn tapped Brooks on the shoulder. "May I cut in?"

Brooks smiled. "Okay, little sister, I'll sit this one out with Katie, but you owe me a dance later."

Andrea nodded. She could feel the heat creep up her neck. Winn took her hand and wrapped his other arm around her, pulling her close. She could swear he had stars in his eyes, or maybe the stars were in her eyes. The official fireworks hadn't started outside, but they were exploding inside—her heart popped like a firecracker. *Wow, just wow! I've never felt like this before.*

"Grab your partner and get ready for a 'Good Time' line dance."

"I'm not sure about line dancing," Winn said.

Andrea grabbed his hand. It's easy. Just do what I do. "Toe,-step,-heel, toe- step-heel, out-touch-in, out-touch-in, turn." Winn tried to follow but almost fell at the turn. Andrea laughed. "Keep trying. You're doing great." When the dance ended, Andrea asked, "Would you like to get a drink and catch your breath?"

"Sure." Winn put his hand on Andrea's arm and turned her away from the stage.

The lead singer of the band announced, "This next dance is for all the lovers out there. I dedicate this next song, 'The Keeper of the Stars,' to my beautiful wife."

***

"We can catch our breath on this one because it's nice and slow." Winn pulled Andrea close. She leaned her head on his shoulder and he burrowed his face in her hair, inhaling the fresh strawberry scent, relishing the soft, silky locks. He could feel her heart beating in sync with his. *I can't believe how good, how right this feels. Andrea looks and feels like an angel. My heart and mind have been in a whirlwind ever since the day we met. I didn't think I could ever fall in love with anyone after Janae, but here I am. I barely know Andrea, but I think I love her.*

The music stopped, but Winn held tight. He didn't want the moment to end. She pulled away and looked at him with those deep blue eyes. He felt himself sinking, the magnetic force sucking him under for the third time, stealing his breath.

She licked her lips. "Um, let's take a break and get something to drink." Her eyes widened, her lashes flickered, and she looked away.

Yes! She felt it too—chemistry.

At the concession stand, she got a cherry limeade and he got a

Dr. Pepper. They turned to walk away when he bumped into a tall cowboy holding a little girl. The man slapped him on the shoulder. "Winn, how's it going?"

Winn froze. In his peripheral vision, he caught Andrea staring at him. His friend looked back and forth between them. Winn cleared his throat. "Andrea, this is Keith. He's the lineman that came to our rescue after the tornado."

She offered her hand. "Thank you. I don't think I thanked you that night."

Keith looked her up and down appraisingly. "I'm glad everything turned out okay." He winked. "Winn's a great guy."

The little girl reached for Winn, and he hugged her. "Where's Chari?" She patted his face with her chubby little fingers.

Winn could feel his heart stop. His throat constricted. He wished the earth would open up and swallow him whole. Finally he opened his mouth. "She's at home with her grandmother." He took Andrea's arm and steered her into the street. Looking over his shoulder he said, "See you Monday, Keith."

Andrea stopped before they reached the other dancers. "Who is Chari?"

Winn shuffled his feet, looked at the ground, glanced up at the sky, and stared at the band before facing her. "I've been meaning to tell you."

"Tell me now."

"I have a little girl. A daughter."

"A daughter?" She jerked her arm out of his grasp. "And," she choked, "a wife?"

"My wife was killed in an auto accident when Chari was six months old."

She blinked and shook her head. "I'm sorry about your wife, but why didn't you tell me about your daughter?"

"I'm all she has. I have to protect her."

"Protect her? From me?" Her voice elevated two octaves.

"She doesn't have a mother." He rubbed his palm over his face, holding onto his jaw. "I don't want her to get attached to someone just to be disappointed. That could be devastating if it happened too many times."

Lightning flashed from her eyes. "Just how many times has that happened?"

"It hasn't. I mean I haven't really dated anyone. Not more than once or twice."

"Well, we've had one official date," moisture pooled in her eyes, "So adios."

He put his hands on her shoulders. "You're different. You're special."

She jerked back and jabbed her finger into his chest. "Yeah, right. That's why you trusted me enough to be truthful."

She turned to walk away. He grasped her shoulder and pulled her close. "Please . . ." Before he could say another word, she flipped him onto the ground. Looking down at him, she said, "You stay away

94

from me. I don't want to ever see or talk to you again."

Suddenly they were surrounded by a group of rowdy cowboys. One of them slurred, "Hey, shweetie, you want us to take care of him for you?" When the stanger put his hands on her, she kneed him and knocked him to the ground.

"Mind your own business." She waved her hands at the others. "Get away . . . all of you!"

Strong arms wrapped her in a bear hug. A soothing voice said, "It's okay, Nieta. We're here."

Brooks, their dad, and Gramps stood between her and the tanked-up cowboys. "If you know what's good for you, you'll fade away," her dad's deep voice carried a stern warning. He had his belt off, the end looped in his hands, swinging the big trophy buckle back and forth.

Winn got up and pointed at the cowboy on the ground. "Don't ever put your hands on a lady."

"Stop it!" Tears streamed down Andrea's red face. "Stop it and go away!" She glared at Winn. "All of you!" She turned and stormed off, with Abuelo's arm still draped around her shoulders.

When they reached the parking lot, she said, "Will you please take me home?"

"Sure." Abuelo led the way to his pickup. As he pulled onto the highway, he asked, "Do you want to talk about it?"

"No," she sobbed.

***

After determining one of them was sober enough to drive, security came and ushered the disorderly cowboys to their vehicles.

Dustin Travis glowered at Winn. "What do you have to say about this?"

Keith walked up and stood beside Winn. "You okay?"

Winn nodded. "I'm fine. This is Andrea's family."

Keith was a big man, but the three Travis men towered over Winn. "You sure you'll be okay?"

"Yes, go back to your family." He slapped him on the back. "I'll see you Monday."

"I hope so." Keith backed away.

Winn turned to Dustin Travis. "It's kind of a long story."

"We've got all night," Dean Travis, Andrea's Gramps, spoke for the first time.

"Let's get out of the spotlight here," Brooks said. As he walked to the parking area, Winn wondered if they were going to beat him to death where nobody could see. He figured they all packed heat legally with a Texas Concealed Carry License.

Brooks stopped by a big four-wheel club cab. "Go ahead talk, and we'll listen."

Winn took a deep breath. "I have a daughter." The three men stood silent. "I didn't tell Andrea about her." Nobody said anything. "My wife was killed in an accident when Charity was only six months old."

"How old is she now?" Brooks asked.

"Four. My mother helps take care of her. That's why I live with my mom."

Gramps spit his tobacco precariously close to Winn's boot. "So why didn't you tell her?"

"I guess I thought I was protecting Chari." Winn rubbed his face. "I don't want her to get attached to someone and then be disappointed."

"How many times has that happened?" Brooks asked.

"None." He looked at the three Travis men, feeling like he was on trial at the Spanish Inquisition. "I haven't dated anyone more than once or twice."

"My daughter will not be a one-night stand for anybody," Dustin said through clinched teeth.

"I know that, sir." Winn took a deep breath. "I know Andrea is special. I respect and admire her." He shuffled his feet. Should he tell them how he really felt? That he thought he loved her?

"Andrea values honesty above everything else. She's probably done with you for good," Dustin said.

"Why don't you all go back to the family? I'd like to talk to Winn alone," Brooks said.

Once the other men were out of earshot, Brooks asked, "Has Andrea told you about me and Katie?"

"Little things, like you singing in the cowboy church band, your music, your little boy." Winn rolled his shoulders hoping to release the tension.

"I met Katie when she was in first grade. We were sweethearts all through school. When I graduated, I headed to Nashville to make my way in country music. The next year, Katie graduated and headed to Chicago to prepare for the symphony." Brooks took his hat off and ran his fingers through his thick black hair. "The next summer, Katie got pregnant but didn't tell me."

"The boy looks just like you."

"Yes. She didn't come back home because everyone would know he was mine. She told her parents the father was some guy in Chicago. She thought that was best, so our families wouldn't pressure us to get married." Brooks took a bandana handkerchief out of his pocket and wiped the sweat from his brow and his neck. "She came home when her mother had cancer. Austin was six. I was here, too." He paused, taking a deep breath before continuing. "I still loved her. I wanted her and Austin in my life, and I prayed and worked to win her back." He twirled his hat in his hands. "Andrea and Katie had been best friends all through school. When she found out Katie was going to have a baby, supposedly with some other guy, Andrea cut off all contact with her. Andrea is loyal to the core, but when somebody crosses her, she's done with them."

"She and Katie seem to get along okay now."

"This past year has been a time of healing for all of us."

Winn shuffled his feet. "So you think there's any hope for me? You think Andrea will forgive me?"

"I don't know. She and Katie shared everything growing up."

98

Brooks shook his head. "Our older sister Celina used to call Andrea the queen of grudges. She doesn't trust or forgive easily."

"Could you talk to her for me? I mean, since what you went through with Katie, you kind of understand, right?"

Brooks shook his head. "Nope. No way will I interfere and get her wrath all over me." He extended his hand. "I will pray for you. And of course I'll pray for my little sister."

Chapter Ten

Winn drove by the clinic and saw Andrea's pickup parked in the drive. He couldn't see if any lights were back where her bedroom and the kitchen break room were located. He thought about going to the door but couldn't get up the nerve. Instead he took out his cell phone and called. After five rings, it went to voicemail. He hung up and drove on home. Once he reached his ranch, he called again. At the tone he said, "Andrea, I'm sorry I didn't tell you about Charity. Could you please forgive me? Give me another chance?" He took a deep breath. "I think we could be good together."

God, you know I'm not much of a praying man, but I'll give it my best shot. He knelt in the barn beside a barrel of grain. *Andrea is special. I think I love her, but it looks like I blew it. Can you fix it for me, or show me how to fix it?*

***

Andrea listened to the message and then blocked Winn's number. She didn't want to hear his voice again. She didn't want to see him again, ever. She looked at her reflection in the mirror—red, swollen eyes and nose. *He's not worth it. Just when I thought I could trust him. Just when I was starting to like him. Starting to like him? Yes, just starting to like him. Goodbye, so long, another dream over and gone.*

She crawled back in bed and curled into a fetal position under the covers. She tried not to cry, but the tears continued to flow, followed by heart-shredding sobs.

***

Abuelo waited on the porch swing until the rest of the family arrived home. "Andrea went to her clinic. She wouldn't tell me nothing about what happened."

Carmella told her father what she knew. "Too bad. I liked the young man." Her downcast eyes reflected sadness.

Dustin said, "It doesn't matter whether we liked him or not, he done bit the bullet."

"You want to take back your bet on a wedding in six months?" Gramps asked.

Abuelo grinned and shook his head. "I think the bet is still on. You didn't see how much she cried. A heart that doesn't care doesn't hurt." He stood and stretched. "I can sleep well now that I know he didn't do nothing bad."

"He didn't tell her the truth. That's bad enough," Dustin said.

Abuelo shrugged. "Aw, not telling everything is not the same as not telling the truth."

Carmella hugged her father. "That may be true for you, but I don't think Andrea will see it that way."

***

Waiting until Austin was in bed, out of earshot, Brooks told

Katie how the evening had unfolded. "Winn seemed like a nice guy, but you know how Andrea feels about honesty."

"Of all people, I know." She kissed her husband and patted his cheek. "I'll talk to her tomorrow."

He raised his eyebrows. "Tread lightly. Your relationship is still not as strong as it used to be."

She laughed. "I know Andrea. I will lend a listening ear."

"Don't expect her to say too much. She's pretty closed-mouthed. I feel like she's hiding something."

"Exactly." Katie turned back the comforter on their bed. "I can understand her reaction when she thought I had been unfaithful to you and broke your heart—you're her brother after all. But from what you said, I think her reaction tonight was way over the top. It's time she opens up and gets it off her chest—whatever *it* is."

***

The next morning when Andrea didn't show up at church, Carmella told her husband, "I'm going outside to call our daughter."

He held on to her hand. "Leave her alone. You can check on her after church."

"What if something happened to her? I need to call."

Dustin shook his head. "How long was she away at school? And how often did you talk to her?"

"At least once a week, but that was different. Nobody broke her heart then."

"We don't know that. We don't know anything about her time

102

at school, except the grades she made." He let go of her hand and put his arm around her. "You can call her after church, but don't ask too many questions. We raised a strong, independent daughter. She'll talk if and when she's ready."

***

Following church services, Brooks and Katie joined his family for dinner. Austin asked, "Where's Aunt Andrea? I didn't see her at church."

Katie broke the silence. "Maybe she's tired after the dance last night. Or maybe she got a call and had to take care of a horse, a cow, or a dog." She tousled her son's hair. "After we eat, I'll take her a plate of food."

"Can I go with you?" Austin batted his long dark eyelashes.

"Why don't you spend some time with me and the new twins—the little colt and filly?" Abuelo flashed his great-grandson a broad smile.

"I'd like that!" Austin beamed.

While cleaning off the table, Carmella asked, "Do you want me to go with you?"

Katie shook her head. "No, I'm hoping we can talk about what happened last night." She began rinsing the dishes. "I can kind of see Winn's point of view."

"Be careful. I don't think Andrea will be interested in the other side of the story." Carmella wrapped foil on the plate of food and slipped it in a quilted carrier. "Go on now and take this to her before it gets cold. I can finish the dishes."

***

Katie prayed as she drove to Andrea's clinic. She loved her sister-in-law and hoped they could once again become best friends, trusting and confiding in one another.

It took a few minutes before Andrea answered the buzzer. "You missed a great service at church. The music was awesome." No response. "Dinner was delicious, so I brought you some of your mom's green chili enchiladas."

"Thanks. I'll put them in the fridge for later." She took the plate and lowered her head.

"So, may I come in?"

"Maybe another time." Andrea lifted her shoulder in a half shrug.

"Do you have any coffee or tea, hot or cold? Either one's okay with me."

"Katie, I know what you're doing, and I don't want to talk about it." She lifted her chin, her facial muscles twitching tightly.

Katie tilted her head, but Andrea looked away. "We don't have to talk about last night. I just want to talk, like we used to. I miss you."

"We talk, but it will never be like it used to be." Tears pooled in her blood shot eyes.

Katie stepped forward and wrapped her in a bear hug. "I love you, Andrea. I'm sorry for hurting you, for hurting Brooks and Austin, and our families. At the time, I thought I was making the right decision." Tears pooled in her eyes. "Things can never be the same, but they can be better, now that we're adults, and we really are sisters now."

Andrea stiffened and pulled away. "No, we are not real sisters." She turned her back. "Go back to your husband and son, and leave me alone."

Katie felt like she'd been slapped in the face. "You're never alone. You have a family who loves you." Andrea turned her back, walked through the lobby, and closed the door. "And you have God."

Tears blurred Katie's vision as she drove back to T-C Quarter Horse Ranch. *God, that didn't turn out the way I planned. Please heal her hurting heart.*

***

When her mother called later that evening, Andrea said she was tired and just needed some time alone. "I don't want anyone to mention Winn. He is nothing, was nothing."

"So it's over?" Carmella asked tentatively.

"There was never anything to begin with." Andrea sighed. "He kept me company during the tornado. He helped some with the clinic. We went out to dinner . . . once. We had a few dances. Yes, it's all over." She let out a harsh breath. "Please don't call again. I'll see you Sunday." She hung up the phone and cried herself to sleep.

Later that evening, Carmella dabbed her eyes as she related

the story to her husband.

Dustin crossed his arms over his broad chest. "I ought to go over there and turn her over my knee and paddle her—something I probably should have done a long time ago."

"You can't do that. She's a grown woman."

"Then she needs to act like it." He spread out his arms and his wife stepped into his embrace.

Hugging him like her life depended on it, she said, "Leave her alone, and she'll come home."

***

Tuesday Andrea sat at her computer working on her pitiful accounts. "In the Garden" played on her phone. She didn't feel like talking to her mother so she let it go to voicemail. The message said, "Brooks is taking Katie to the hospital in Lubbock. Your dad and I have Austin. We plan to leave in about an hour. That should give them time to get settled in, but we can wait for you if you're available."

She wanted to go, but she didn't want to ride with her parents. She finished her online banking, changed clothes, and headed down the highway. Her stomach rumbled. The salad she ate for lunch had worn off, so she stopped at Dairy Queen and got a Chocolate Xtreme Blizzard. Images of Winn eating a Banana Split Blizzard flashed in her mind, and she shook her head. *No, I won't let you invade my thoughts today, or tomorrow, or ever.*

As she drove down the highway, she thought about the baby,

wondered if he would have the Cordova, Castilian blue eyes and black hair or hazel eyes and auburn hair like Katie. She loved babies, all kinds of babies, except rats and snakes. She had watched animals be born but never a real live baby. She would love to see this baby's birth, but they probably wouldn't want her in the delivery room, even if it was allowed, not after the way she treated Katie on Sunday.

Her parents, Austin, and Katie's parents were in the waiting room when she got to the hospital. "Are Abuelo and Gramps here?" Andrea asked.

Her mother shook her head. "Things were different for the older generation. They will come see the baby after he's born."

Andrea gave Austin a hug. "So, how you feeling little man?"

"I'm good." He put his arm around her neck and pulled her close. "I missed you. Did you miss me?"

She ran her fingers through his thick, black hair. "Always."

He showed her pictures he had drawn. "This is me holding baby Dallas."

Andrea smiled. "Aww, you think he will have black hair like yours?"

"Yep, and like yours and my dad and Abuela and Abuelo."

"I think I'll go back and see how things are coming along," Donna Kane said.

"I'll go with you," Richard said, taking his wife's hand.

Andrea watched them walk through the double doors. Donna's cancer was in remission, but she still seemed weak and fragile. She looked at her own mother, vibrant, healthy, and strong. Her father had gained weight, and his health had improved the past year since he retired from the rodeo circuit. Her grandfathers were healthy and strong. They certainly didn't act like senior citizens. She thought about Winn, losing his dad when he was only sixteen, then losing his wife when the baby was just six months old. Her throat constricted. She shook her head and pinched the bridge of her nose to restrict the tears that threatened her eyes.

Austin wrinkled his nose and asked, "Don't you like this picture?"

She hadn't realized he was showing her another drawing. She took the paper. "Yes, I like all your pictures."

"This is me and you, cause you might not want to hold Dallas."

"I love you so much." She hugged him. "I would like to hold Dallas because I didn't get to hold you when you were little." He crawled on her lap and hugged her. She realized he was feeling a bit insecure about the new baby. She knew all about insecurity. She patted his head and whispered in his ear, "You will always be my number one nephew."

The Kanes returned. "Carmella, would you like to go in? The nurse said it shouldn't be too long now," Donna said.

Carmella asked her husband, "You sure you don't want to go in?"

"Nah, you go ahead."

When Carmella returned, she said, "Andrea, you can go in and see Brooks and Katie if you'd like."

Austin jumped up. "Can I go?"

Dustin stood and extended his hand. "Why don't we go downstairs and get an ice cream? Richard, you want to go with us?"

"Ya, I've sat about as long as I can stand."

Andrea watched them get into the elevator. Turning to her mother, she asked, "You think it would be okay to go in and see Katie?"

Carmella nodded. "She asked for you."

Andrea walked in the private room to witness Katie groan and push, perspiration beaded on her red face. When the contraction subsided, Andrea patted her shoulder and said, "I'm praying for you."

The doctor walked in and examined her. "You're doing great—almost there."

"I'll see you later." Andrea stopped at the door, turned, and said, "I love you, Katie."

The doctor said, "Anybody else coming in before we lock the door?"

Brooks asked, "Andrea, you want to stay?"

She shook her head. Watching an animal give birth was much different than witnessing the pain of a person, someone you loved like a sister

Shortly Brooks came out carrying the baby wrapped in a blue hospital blanket. "I would like to introduce Dallas Roberto Travis."

109

Brooks said, smiling from ear to ear.

Carmella cupped her face with her hands. "Abuelo will be so happy he's named after him."

"Austin's middle name is Richard. Dustin and Dean don't sound right with Dallas, so we named him after Abuelo." Brooks pulled off the knitted baby hat. "Roberto is a perfect name for somebody with all that black hair."

Austin asked, "Can I hold him now?"

Brooks tousled his hair. "Not yet, Pardner. In an hour or so, when they take your mom to a regular room, then you can." He tried to put the hat back on the baby. Andrea stepped up, kissed the baby on the head, and covered the thick black hair with the hat.

"If you all go get something to eat, can you bring me something? Katie was already having contractions before lunch, and I couldn't eat. Now I feel like I could eat a side of beef."

"What would you like, Son?" Dustin asked.

"Anything, just food."

"They have pizza downstairs," Austin's violet eyes sparkled.

"Maybe not pizza. I need something more substantial, more meat."

"We'll see what they have, and I can text you the choices and bring it right up," Andrea said.

"No, I can wait until you're finished eating. Maybe by then Katie will be in a room."

The hospital cafeteria was more like the food court at a mall.

Andrea and Austin ate pizza. The parents ate from the buffet. After they finished, Andrea said, "Austin, why don't we go to the gift shop and see if we can get something for your mom and Dallas."

"We would like to get her flowers," Donna said.

Andrea laughed. "Okay, we won't buy flowers."

Austin selected a stuffed horse for Dallas and a box of chocolates for his mother. "I want to get something for you, too, to celebrate your first day as a big brother."

He walked around the shop, looking, touching, and finally selected another stuffed horse. "If I get this, I can play with Dallas. My mom said babies need soft stuff cause they're soft. I want the brown one, like my mom's horse Sissy, and I'll give Dallas the palomino like your horse Princess."

"You are the sweetest boy ever. Dallas is so lucky to have you for a big brother." Andrea hugged him. "And I am so lucky to have you as my nephew." *Katie and Brooks are lucky—no, they're blessed to have each other and two beautiful, healthy little boys.*

After Katie was settled in a room, everyone took turns holding Dallas. Andrea felt euphoric holding the new little life in her arms. She wanted a baby, babies, someday, but first she would have to find the right man.

Chapter Eleven

Wednesday evening Winn's mother said, "You've been walking around on your bottom lip all week. What's wrong?"

"Nothing." He focused on loading the dishwasher.

Faith handed him a bowl. "Did something happen with the cookie lady?"

"The candy lady makes the cookies." He methodically slipped the silverware in the slots. "Nothing happened with her."

"Oh, that's right." She turned off the water and began wiping the counter. "The cookie/candy lady is your *friend's* mother." She stood with her hands on her hip. "So what happened with your friend?"

He slipped a detergent tablet in the holder and slammed the door. "I'm sorry." He patted the dishwasher and started the wash cycle.

Faith put her hand on her son's arm. "The dishwasher doesn't have feelings, but you're wearing yours on your shoulders for all the world to see."

"The world doesn't care about my feelings, Mom."

She glanced through the door to check on Charity who was watching *Veggie Tales*. She motioned to the table. "Sit with me awhile."

"I really don't want to talk about it." He shrugged his shoulders. "There's nothing to talk about."

She raised her eyebrows. "Indulge me a few minutes." She filled a measuring cup with water. "Would you like a cup of coffee?"

"No, I couldn't sleep for sure if I drank coffee this late."

She put water in the teapot. "You want tea or hot chocolate?"

"No, thanks."

She made herself a cup of herbal tea. "Judging by the circles under your eyes, you haven't been sleeping too well anyway. Maybe a cup of warm milk?" He shook his head.

She sat across from him. "For seventeen years I lived with a man who barely talked to me, never shared his feelings, or listened to mine."

"Mom, please. I don't want to talk about anything heavy right now."

She raised her chin. "I tried to raise you better. You and I had long talks about deep thoughts, feelings, opinions, heavy stuff." She sipped her tea. "After your dad died, instead of pulling together, I felt you pull away. I know you were angry with me for selling the bulls, but I wanted to protect you. You were all I had." She picked up a napkin and dabbed at the tears in her eyes. "I realize now that I have been overprotective, domineering, controlling."

"No, you've been a good mom." He hated it when she cried. "You can't be everything—mom, dad, best friend, rock, and grandmother." He drummed his fingers on the table. "You have to realize I'm a man. I need to stand on my own two feet, pull myself up by the bootstraps, get back in the saddle, take care of business, and all the other clichés Dad used to drill into my head." He lifted his gaze. "You can't fight my battles. This isn't something you can fix."

She bobbed her head. "I understand." She reached across and rested her hand on his fingers. "I do have something to tell you."

"What's wrong?"

"Nothing." She withdrew her hand and ran her finger over the rim of her cup before looking up. "You know my boss, Sam Howard?"

Winn's jaw tightened. "Has he been giving you a hard time?"

Shaking her head, she carried her cup to the sink. "No nothing like that." Leaning against the counter she said, "Actually, it's just the opposite. He has been kind and considerate," she paused before continuing, "and very attentive."

Winn shuffled his feet under the table. "Attentive? In a good way?"

"I think so." She rinsed her cup and returned to the table. "We've had lunch together several times. I enjoy his company, and I wanted to tell you before taking it to the next level."

"The next level?"

"Yes, as in dating." She lowered her eyes, which made the blush more prominent.

He walked to the door and peeked to see Charity still

engrossed in her video. Turning back to his mother, he said, "Well, I didn't see that one coming." He leaned over and hugged her. "If this makes you happy, then I'm happy."

She patted his arm. "Right now I'm happy."

"He better treat you right, the way you deserve to be treated." He stretched and yawned.

"You deserve happiness, too." She stood and kissed her son on the cheek. "But you can't be happy if you keep everything bottled up."

Winn didn't have anyone to talk to about his feelings. Monday Keith had asked about the dance and "the girl vet." The linemen were a bunch of good guys. He felt closer to Keith than anyone else at work, but it wasn't a touchy, feely kind of relationship. Winn said he had spent some time with Andrea, but it didn't work out—no big deal. Keith raised his eyebrows questioningly but let the subject drop.

Maybe he should talk to his mom. The feelings swirling inside felt like they might explode. He told her about meeting someone in the tornado, helping her with cleanup and rebuilding, going to dinner in Lubbock, then part of what happened at the dance. He didn't mention her name. Or her family's name. Or that she is the vet who took over Doc Mitchell's practice.

His mother's brow puckered. "I understand your motives, but I can understand her feeling like you didn't care enough to tell her about the most important thing in your life." She sighed heavily. "If it's meant to be, it will work out. If she stays mad over something like

115

this, then you're better off without her." Despite the warmth of the kitchen, she shivered. "I never knew when your dad was going to be happy go lucky or get mad and explode. It's a terrible way to live." She dabbed the tears pooling in her eyes. "As much as you're hurting now, I'd hate to see you end up with a moody, pouty puss." She made eye contact and held it. "Charity certainly doesn't need to be around someone who would fly off the handle over every little thing."

"She's not like that. I don't think this is a little thing." Winn rubbed his chin. "I should have told her."

"Yes, you should have, but you didn't." She shrugged. "We all do things we shouldn't. We acknowledge our wrong-doing and ask for forgiveness. People who can't forgive become bitter. I should know. I held on to bitterness against your dad until it almost ate me up. After you went away to college, I went to a Christian counselor in Lubbock. With his help and prayer, I asked God to forgive me and help me forgive your father. I could never think about a relationship with another man until I dealt with the past and left it there."

Charity came into the kitchen. "My video is over. Can I watch another one?"

Winn hugged his daughter. "It's bath time. Then story time. Then bed time."

***

Long after he put Charity to bed, Winn lay awake thinking about everything his mother said. Deep down he knew he harbored bitterness against Janae. She shouldn't have been drinking and

116

driving, especially not with their baby in the car. His anger at Janae's parents went even deeper. They spoiled their daughter, dressed her like a doll, put her on display, but never really made her feel loved for the person she was inside instead of how she looked. They let him know he wasn't good enough for their daughter, not because of any character flaw, but because he didn't have a blueblood pedigree and the money to go with it. Janae probably chose him to spite her parents. The ultimate insult was when they tried to take his daughter away from him.

He quit the rodeo so they couldn't use that against him. He moved home so his mother could help take care of Charity. He didn't get involved with women for fear Janae's parents would find out and sic their lawyers on him again.

Andrea was different. She was special. He had been cautious. Maybe he wasn't just protecting his daughter. Maybe he was protecting his own heart. The fear of rejection ran deep. Yes, he hadn't forgiven his father for his transgressions—the drinking, the anger and verbal abuse against his mother and him, the whippings that felt more like beatings, the absence of love and affirmation.

God I've done a lot of bad things. I've held grudges against people, denied my own feelings, laughed off the hurt rather than dealing with the feelings. Can you forgive me? Can you help me forgive? Mom's right. I'm not ready for a relationship until I unpack my baggage and leave it on the curb. Maybe I should talk to a counselor.

Chapter Twelve

The Sunday after Dallas was born, Abuelo smoked a brisket and the Travis and Kane families took dinner to Katie and Brooks. The grandfathers and great-grandfathers fussed over the new baby and Austin while the two grandmothers spread out the feast. After dinner, the men went out to look at Austin's new calf.

"Andrea, you can sit with Katie while Donna and I clean up. I think you're the only one who hasn't had a chance to hold Dallas," Carmella told her daughter.

Andrea sat in the rocker, and Katie handed her the baby. As she looked in her nephew's face, his midnight blue eyes connected with hers as if he could see into her soul. Snuggling the baby with the rhythmic rocking stirred something deep inside. She would soon be twenty-seven. Her biological clock tick-tocked. She wondered why her older sister Celina hadn't had children yet. She became a teacher because of her love of kids. She would be a great mother.

I wonder if I'll be a good mother, if I ever get to be one. I'll need to work on my short temper before I think about having kids. Of course, I'll need to work on my anger and trust issues before I think about getting married, or even having a relationship.

"How are you feeling, Katie?" She asked, continuing to gaze

118

in the baby's eyes.

"I feel great. It is so much easier this time with all the family around to help. Aunt LeAnn helped when Austin was born, but she was busy with work. People don't realize how many hours of practice the symphony requires." She smiled. "It's been great to have Brooks beside me, giving me emotional support, making me feel loved, treasured, and respected."

Andrea nodded. *Yes, that would be great.*

"I suffered deep, post-partum depression after Austin was born."

Andrea looked up. She couldn't imagine confident Katie ever feeling depressed.

Katie toyed with a lock of hair. "I loved Austin, but I felt ashamed because I wasn't married. I felt guilty because I didn't tell Brooks or my family about him. I felt lonely because I didn't have any real friends." She sighed deeply. "I really missed having you to talk to. Many times I thought about calling you, but I didn't want Brooks to know the truth and feel pressured to marry me."

"But you knew he loved you."

"I loved him too, but I didn't want to stand in the way of his dream." She leaned back in her recliner and closed her eyes. "In my selfishness, I prayed that he would call me and say he was giving up music, that he would rather have me than fame and fortune. When he didn't call, I became angry and bitter. I blamed him for everything."

Andrea looked up and searched her sister-in-law's face. "In

retrospect, don't you think it would have been easier and better just to tell the truth?"

Katie shook her head. "Easier maybe, but not better." She gazed around the room, her eyes settling on their wedding picture. "We are together now because that's what we both want. Brooks had to run his race to realize the prize was right here in West Texas—home, family, and God. I had to shoot for the stars in Chicago to realize family and God are more important than symphony." She clasped her hands in her lap. "We grew up together and took each other for granted. Our time apart helped us mature and realize our relationship is a gift from God. I plan to spend the rest of my life loving Brooks and being the best wife and mother I can be. I still love music, but it is more enjoyable as a hobby than a task master."

"You don't realize how blessed you and Brooks are."

"We are truly blessed. I pray that you will find someone to love and cherish you the way Brooks loves me, someone you can love and respect the way I love him."

Andrea hung her head. "Don't hold your breath on that."

"I know you didn't date much in high school, but wasn't there anyone special in college or vet school?"

Andrea shook her head. Through clenched teeth she said, "I don't want to talk about it."

The baby started straining and fussing. "Sounds like I need to change him and feed him." Katie stood and took Dallas in her arms. "Andrea, we love you, and we're always here if you ever want to talk, about anything."

Donna and Carmella walked in and heard the last statement. After Katie closed the bedroom door, silence hung in the living room punctuated by the clanging pendulum of the clock on the mantle. Andrea stood and stretched. "I've had a busy week, so I think I'll head on home."

Her mother followed her outside. When they reached her pickup, Carmella said, "Andrea, we're all here for you if you need anything."

She opened the door and snapped, "I don't."

Carmella put her hand on her daughter's arm. "I am concerned about your anger. Whatever it is, I think it was there before Winn came along. Don't hold it inside. If you don't want to talk to us, talk to someone."

"Someone, like who?"

"Like the pastor at church."

Andrea shook her head. "I hardly know him."

"That might be a good thing." Carmella nodded. "He seems like a good man."

"I'm not talking to him." Andrea started the vehicle and pulled away from her mother. As she drove back to her clinic, the anger built to boiling. She knew her family meant well, but they didn't know how she felt or why.

That night Andrea lay in bed, staring at the ceiling, trying to shut down her run away thoughts. Finally sleep came, followed by the nightmare. She felt herself sliding into a deep, dark hole. She needed help, but her tongue tangled up behind paralyzed lips. Her limp body collapsed. She felt someone dragging her. She could hear her feet scraping the floor, deafening voices echoed from a tunnel. She was a turkey wishbone being pulled apart until she cracked and fell.

She awoke in a pool of perspiration, her heartbeat thundering out of her chest. Disoriented, she lay still. Where was she? How did she get here? Consciousness filtered through the fog. She touched the soft cotton of her pajama top, rolled over and turned on the light. She reached in her nightstand, pulled out her pistol, and released the safety.

Why did she have the nightmare? Did she hear something? Had she set the alarm before going to bed? The blinking light above the door assured her all was safe. She got out of bed and turned on every light as she walked through the clinic. She turned the lights off in the reception area and peeked through the blinds. Nothing. She turned lights out as she retraced the steps to her room and lay in bed. Nothing was wrong outside. Nothing was wrong inside. But everything was wrong with her. Why was she having the nightmare now, after two years?

She told herself it was okay. It wouldn't happen again. But it did—the next night, and the next. Wednesday she called her mother. "What are you having for supper?"

"Chicken fried steak. Would you like to join us?"

"Yes, I'd like that. I'll see you around six." She hadn't talked to anyone in her family since Sunday, but she knew she always had a place at their table. She needed the company, someone to talk with, to laugh with, to feel safe with.

After dinner, she asked, "Abuelo, will you play and sing for me?"

"Anything for you, Nieta." He stood and walked to the door. "Make a playlist while I go get my guitar."

"Would you like me to play, too?" Carmella asked. "The dishes can wait."

"If you want to play," Dustin said, "I can do the dishes."

Wow, just wow. Andrea had never known of her father helping with dishes. Do miracles never cease? *God is still in the miracle business.* The words from the pastor's sermon echoed in her mind.

Andrea sat on the porch swing next to Gramps while her mother and Abuelo tuned their guitars. Abuleo began singing "Baby Face"—the song he had always sung for her since she was the baby of the family. "You'll always be my baby face, but now that you're all grown up, this song might be more fitting," and he sang "The Most Beautiful Girl in the World" followed by "Hey Good Lookin".

Gramps asked him to sing "Georgia" and Andrea wondered why he had never married after his wife, Georgia, died so young.

Her mother sang "Sweet Dreams" sounding just like Patsy Cline. Andrea wished she had sweet dreams instead of the nightmares that haunted her. Next she sang "Crazy" and Andrea wondered why she felt crazy. It had nothing to do with Winn. They didn't love each other. He hadn't left her for someone new, but there was someone in his past he loved. She wondered if she was crazy for crying over something that happened in her past, something she thought she had worked through in counseling. Maybe she needed to find a counselor in Lubbock to help her get over the nightmares.

Dustin joined the group. A big fan of George Strait, he asked for "Amarillo by Morning". When Abuelo stopped singing, Dustin leaned over and whispered in his wife's ear, "I'm so glad I didn't lose you during my wandering days. Thanks for loving me." He kissed her and asked, "Roberto, would you sing "I Cross My Heart"?

Andrea swiped at the tears as she remembered listening to those songs with Winn, and she wondered if she would ever find true love.

Let's end with "Amazing Grace" Carmella said, closing her eyes and singing the song with sincere passion.

"Thanks, everyone." Andrea kissed her grandparents and parents. "I'm really tired. Would it be okay if I stayed here tonight?"

"Of course. Our home will always be your home," Carmella said.

Gramps stood and spit tobacco over the porch rail. "Has that Winn guy been giving you trouble?"

Andrea shook her head rapidly. "No, I haven't even seen him. He tried to call, but I blocked his number." She pinched the bridge of her nose. "I'm tired, but if you're going to worry about me if I stay here, then I'll go on home."

"No, no, we want you to stay." Her mother hugged her.

"I don't want you to worry because I'm okay. Really."

***

After she went inside, Dustin asked, "You think this is about Winn?"

Carmella shook her head. "I am worried."

"I wouldn't mind working the guy over," Gramps said, spitting tobacco.

Abuelo said, "I think she has much anger. I saw it when Katie first came home. It's more than Winn."

"What can we do?" Carmella looked from one man to another.

Dustin said, "Roberto, you're the wise one. What do you think?"

"Love her. Give her space, but be there for her if she falls."

"I don't want her to fall," Carmella said.

"Every bird has to leave the nest. Falling is part of life." Roberto hugged his daughter. "If she didn't leave the nest, you would be ready to push her out."

"I don't think so." Carmella went inside and finished putting the dishes away that her husband had washed. She noticed the light in Andrea's room, so she knocked on the door. "May I come in?"

"I'm already in bed."

Carmella opened the door. "You know what I miss most now that you kids are grown?" Andrea shook her head. "I miss reading to

125

you at night, praying with you before bedtime."

"You didn't even do that when we were teenagers."

"No, but I wanted to." Carmella sat on the edge of the bed. "It has been wonderful having Austin here. It brings back such fond memories."

"You've been a great mom. Letting go is part of that."

"I don't think a mother ever completely lets go of her children, no matter how old they are." Carmella tucked her hair behind her ear. "I will always love you and be here . . . if you need me."

"Thanks, Mom." She reached over and turned out the light. "Good night. I'll see you in the morning."

Carmella stood. "Is there anything special you would like for breakfast?"

"Oatmeal, the real stuff, with cinnamons and apples?"

She laughed. "You can have anything, and you want oatmeal?"

"It brings back fond memories of ordinary days."

***

Andrea lay awake wondering if the nightmares would come into this room, the safe place where she grew up, with her parents just down the hall. Oatmeal? She sighed. Yes, she needed simple comfort food to fill the emptiness deep inside.

She recited the Twenty-third Psalm and prayed. *Lord, you are the Good Shepherd, and I am the sheep that lost its way. My soul needs restored. You promise to walk through the valley with me, but the evil scares me to death. I don't want a table in the presence of my enemies. I don't want to face them, not even in my dreams. I just want your goodness and mercy.*

After the darkness of sleep overtook her, the nightmare came again. Paralyzed with fear, her mouth opened and sound emerged, a bloodcurdling scream. Light flooded the tunnel. Footsteps pounded. Hands touched her, big strong hands. She willed her arms to flail, to fight back through the fog.

"Andrea, it's okay. I'm here. I won't let anything hurt you." Her father wrapped his arms around her and she sobbed into his chest. He held her until she was cried out. She pulled away and lay back on her pillow.

"I had a nightmare." She saw the anguish on her mother's face. "I'm okay now. Thanks."

"How long have you been having nightmares?" Her father asked.

She shrugged.

"I saw my mother thrown and stomped by a horse. We were riding out together, to take lunch to the branding crew." Her dad rubbed his eyes with his hands. "I was just a kid, and it scared me to death. I didn't want to leave her, but I knew she needed help. She was breathing, but it was labored. I don't know how long I waited until I finally got on my horse and rode back to ranch headquarters. We were probably closer to the crew, but they didn't have a phone to call for a doctor." He stood and stretched. With his back to her, he said, "My mom was dead by the time we got back. I felt guilty, and I thought my dad blamed me. I had nightmares, too."

"When did the nightmares stop?" Andrea whispered.

"I had them every night for a while. My dad finally took me to a doctor in town. If they had counselors back then, we didn't know about it." He sat beside her and took her hand. "The doctor told Dad we needed to talk about my mom, talk about the good memories. I needed to know that what happened wasn't my fault, and he didn't blame me." He pinched the bridge of his nose—maybe that's where her habit came from. "My dad talked to me more the next few months than he had the rest of his life. Mom grew up in a small town in Georgia. They met when he was in the army. He felt guilty for taking her to the ranch." Sitting on the side of her bed, he said, "You know that George Jones song 'He Stopped Loving Her Today'?" She nodded. "That's my dad—as tough as nails on the outside, soft as a baby on the inside. He won't stop loving my mom until the day he dies."

Her mother sat on the other side of the bed. "Do you want to talk about your nightmares? To help them go away?"

She shook her head. "No, I'm okay. Really it's not that bad." She forced a smile, but she knew they could tell it was fake. "I'm sorry I woke you. Please try to go back to sleep."

Carmella hugged her. "We're right down the hall if you need us."

"Thanks. Goodnight." After they were gone, she got up and closed the door so they couldn't hear her cry. Yes, she needed to talk to someone, but not her family. She didn't want any of them to end up in prison for murder.

Chapter Thirteen

Two weeks later Andrea had an appointment with a counselor in Lubbock. After giving her information to the receptionist, she sat and thumbed through a magazine. The door of the counselor's office opened, and Winn walked into the lobby. Andrea could hear him set up an appointment for two weeks.

He did a double take when he saw Andrea. The receptionist said, "Ms. Travis, the counselor will see you now."

Andrea followed Winn out the door. "What are you doing here?"

"I could ask you the same thing, but I figure it's none of my business."

"Are you stalking me?"

"In case you didn't notice, I was here before you. Maybe you're stalking me."

"Don't flatter yourself." She put her hand on the door knob and said, "I told you to stay away from me."

He put his hands up in surrender. "You think I want to be humiliated again by one of your Karate moves?"

She shook her head and left him standing in the hall. The counselor stood in his doorway, extended his hand, and said, "Andrea, it's nice to meet you. Please come in and have a seat."

Sitting in the chair in front of his black, modern desk, she felt like a little girl called into the principal's office for fighting on the playground. His penetrating eyes sized her up. Finally he said, "Tell me about yourself."

"About why I'm here?"

"We can start there if you'd like."

"Why was Winn Timberman here?"

"I'm sorry, but I can't discuss one client with another."

She crossed her arms over her chest. "I'm not officially a client."

He nodded. "Professional ethics demands confidentiality."

"Which means you won't tell him anything I say?"

"Of course not."

She uncrossed her arms and ran her palms down her thighs. "I've started having nightmares again." She told him about the nightmares.

"When did they start, and how long has it been from the time they stopped until they started again?"

"Two years."

He arched his eyebrows. "Did something happen to precipitate the nightmares?"

She took a deep breath and began. "When I was in vet school, I met a guy—good-looking, smart, outgoing personality—lots of money. He had a reputation as a player, so I wasn't interested in him.

He chose me as his lab partner." She clenched and unclenched her fists. "While we worked together, he was a perfect gentleman. He kept asking me out, and I kept turning him down. We went to lunch together with a group of other students. Then we went to dinner a few times, in a group. He invited me to a club to hear a classmate's band." She paused, taking a deep breath. "I don't drink alcohol, ever. I had a couple of soft drinks and needed to go to the restroom." She swiped at the tears pooling in her eyes. "When I came back to our table, my glass had been refilled. Being naïve about the party scene, I didn't think anything about it." She shuddered and closed her eyes. "We were dancing when I felt numb, dazed, like floating out of my body. I tried to talk, but my speech was so slurred, I couldn't even understand myself. I felt myself slipping, losing consciousness."

The counselor handed her a box of tissues, and she wiped at the free-flowing tears. She took deep breaths trying to regain control before continuing.

"The next day I woke up in a strange bed, and I was terrified because I couldn't remember what happened or how I got there. A couple of girls in my class saw the guy practically dragging me out of the club, and they intervened." Her speech sped up along with her heartbeat. "He told them I had too much to drink, so he was taking me home. They didn't know I didn't drink, but they told him they would call the police if he tried to take me out in that condition." She trembled. "Thank God he passed me off to them at the mention of the police." She rubbed her arms. "They took me to their apartment so I

132

could sleep it off."

The counselor nodded. "I'm glad your friends rescued you before he could assault you."

"They were acquaintances, not friends. I spent the day limp, confused, and sick to my stomach. I should have gone to the emergency room to have a blood test to determine what he slipped into my drink. I could have died."

"Did you ever find out what he gave you?"

"I researched date rape drugs and figured it out." She rolled her shoulders. "Vets and vet students have access to Ketamine, which is used as an anesthetic for animals. Druggies will break in and steal it from veterinarian clinics to use for colorful highs. It's a great date rape drug because it's fast acting, colorless, tasteless, and metabolizes quickly, which makes detection difficult."

"Did you report it?"

She shook her head. "I couldn't prove it."

"Did you tell anyone?"

Her shoulders sagged. "I went to a counselor because the nightmares kept me from sleeping. She gave me sleeping pills, antidepressants, and taught me relaxation techniques. After a few months of counseling, I quit having nightmares, so I stopped taking the pills and stopped going to see her."

"When did the nightmares begin again?"

She wiped her eyes and blew her nose. "A few weeks ago."

"Did something happen to trigger them?"

"Winn Timberman."

"What did he do?"

She crossed her legs and began kicking her foot. "I thought you couldn't talk about one client to another."

"This session is about you."

She rubbed her hands on her jeans and told him how they met and what had transpired.

The counselor steepled his fingers. "Why do you think that caused the nightmares?"

"Because I thought I could trust him, but I couldn't!" Her harsh voice was louder than she intended.

He nodded. "From what you've told me, it doesn't sound like he intentionally did anything to hurt you."

"He didn't tell me the truth."

"Do you have trust issues with other people? Significant people in your life?"

"Not with my family." She shook her head. "We're not perfect, but we are close, loving, and supportive." She hesitated, took a deep breath, and continued, "My best friend forever lied to me, to my brother, to my family and hers." She told him the story about Katie, Brooks, and Austin.

"Have you forgiven her?"

"Yes." She rolled her shoulders again. "Maybe not. Not completely."

"Do you trust yourself?"

She hung her head. "No. I'm afraid to trust my own judgement."

The counselor sat with a contemplative expression on his face. In a soft, reassuring voice he said, "That's where we need to begin." He took out a notebook, wrote something on the top, and handed it to her. "Your homework this week is to write down everything you have done right in your life, every good decision you've made, everything you have accomplished, and every goal you have achieved. Only positive thoughts and actions go in this notebook, nothing negative." He opened his desk drawer and took out a prescription pad. "I'm writing you a prescription for sleeping pills."

She shook her head. "No, I don't want to take pills."

"Just for one week to take the edge off so you can sleep. We'll talk about it again next week." He stood and walked her to the door. He said to his receptionist, "Can we squeeze Ms. Travis in next week?"

Andrea said, "I don't want to come in when Mr. Timberman is here. I don't want to see him."

The receptionist glanced at the doctor, and said, "Of course."

Chapter Fourteen

Winn thought about Andrea as he left the doctor's office. He wondered what made her so angry and why she went to see a counselor.

After dinner and putting Charity to bed, he sat in the kitchen with his mother. "I liked the counselor you recommended."

She nodded and poured hot water over her chamomile tea.

"How long did you see him?" he asked as he stirred sugar into his iced tea.

"Twice a month for a couple of months, then once a month for a few months. He helped me see through my anger and bitterness, how to focus on the positives instead of the negatives."

"How are things going with you and your boss?"

"I feel like I'm sixteen again, only wiser." She smiled. "When I met your father at the Fourth of July rodeo, he was handsome and charming, wild and exciting. He called me and sent postcards from all the places he went. It seemed so much more fun than living on a farm. My step-mother and I never got along. I felt like Cinderella and her two daughters were the little princesses. As soon as I graduated from high school, your dad and I ran off and got married. By then he was making a name for himself and making money. It was a wild ride, and we did have some good times. The year he won the world

136

championship, we bought this ranch. Each year, he added more stock." She sipped her tea. "He wanted to win the world title one more time, but instead he kept slipping in the ratings. I wanted him to retire before he got hurt. Of course that only added to our problems."

"So you loved him?"

"I loved him madly." She patted her son's hand. "He loved us, too, but he was so intense. He had more energy and passion than he could control."

"Let's talk about your boss."

"You can refer to him as Sam." She leaned back in her chair, making eye contact. "His wife died of an aneurysm, and his girls are married and gone. He is stable, and we enjoy each other's company. It was a bit awkward going to church with him because his wife was involved in all the women's organizations. I think this week we're going to visit the county cowboy church."

Winn choked on his iced tea. He stood, turning his back to her, and poured the remainder of his tea in the kitchen sink.

She stood and patted him on the back. "Are you alright?"

He nodded and picked up the dish cloth to wipe off the tea he had spewed on the table.

"Would you and Charity like to go to cowboy church with us?"

He shook his head. "I don't want to crowd in on you."

"The way things are moving along, I'd like him to meet you and Charity soon."

"He knows me from work."

"I mean more of a personal level."

"Not this Sunday." He kissed his mother on the cheek. "Goodnight."

Winn wondered if he should tell his mother that Andrea and her family attended the cowboy church. Nope, no reason to do that. From what he's heard, it's a big church—easy to get lost in the crowd.

***

After church on Sunday, Sam Howard saw an old friend standing by the band members at the back of the church. "Richard Kane, it's been a long time." He addressed Faith. "We were almost family. My brother Donald dated Richard's sister LeAnn in high school." He put his hand on her back. "This is my friend Faith Timberman."

Richard introduced his wife Donna, his daughter Katie, and her husband Brooks. Dustin Travis introduced himself and asked, "Are you related to Stony Timberman?"

"Yes, he was my husband," Faith said.

"He was one of the greatest bull riders ever." Dustin shook her hand.

"Yes, he was."

Carmella Travis said, "Faith it is very nice to meet you." Andrea joined the group, and Carmella said, "This is our daughter Andrea. This is Faith *Timberman*."

Faith extended her hand, but Andrea stood paralyzed. Katie

stepped forward and shook Faith's hand. Turning to Sam, she asked, "Your brother is *the* Donald Howard my Aunt LeAnn fell in love with?"

He chuckled. "I don't know about that. He loved her, but she broke his heart when she went off to Chicago."

Katie nodded. "I understand he made it big in the oil business and lives in Houston."

"Yep, he succeeded at everything he tried, except love."

Katie wondered what that meant but thought it would be rude to ask.

Richard said, "I see your name every time we get the County Co-op magazine in the mail."

Andrea took advantage of the conversation and slipped out the door.

***

As she drove back to her clinic, Andrea could still feel the heat of the blush on her neck and face. She wondered if Winn told his mother about her. The woman didn't show any emotion at the introduction. No, he probably didn't tell his mother. He was probably deceptive to her, too.

She called and left a message on the answering machine at her parents' house telling them she had work she needed to do and wouldn't be able to join them for dinner. She was sure they would have questions she didn't want to answer.

As she ate her salad and yogurt, she read through her notebook

139

of positive accomplishments. She had worked hard in school, earned a scholarship, graduated at the top of her class. She was a good daughter, sister, and granddaughter. She had been a loyal, best friend forever to Katie until she broke up with Brooks and betrayed everyone who loved her. Andrea had never had another close friend. In college and vet school she concentrated on her studies. She had never had a real boyfriend, no close relationships with any males except family. Did that mean there was something wrong with her?

She had a normal attraction to guys. In high school all the guys she knew were walking hormones. She added to the notebook: "I made good choices in high school." In college guys were party animals. She wrote: "I made good choices in college." Then in vet school there was Hunter, who preyed on weak women. She didn't fall into his trap, so he tried to seduce her with Ketamine. She added another entry: "I am a fighter and a survivor. I can defend myself. I have a black belt. I made good choices in vet school." In large block letters she wrote: "I AM NOT RESPONSIBLE FOR THE WRONG CHOICES OF OTHERS!!!"

On the next page in bold, curly, calligraphy she wrote: "I am a strong person. I am smart. I can trust myself. I am Andrea Travis, DVM."

***

While eating dinner with her parents, Katie said, "Tell me about Donald Howard."

"That's your aunt's story to tell, not ours," her father

140

answered.

"Aunt LeAnn told me a little bit. Do you know she still loves him?"

Her father ignored her and said, "Austin, you and your dad want to ride in the mule with me while I check on the cattle?"

After they left, Katie stared at her mother. "Mom?"

As they cleared the table and did dishes, her mother said, "Donald and LeAnn were a couple years ahead of me in school. He was the captain of the basketball team and the six-man football team. They were voted homecoming queen and king, Valentine sweethearts, cutest couple, most likely to succeed."

"I guess they did succeed, just not together."

"His father was an oilfield worker. LeAnn had bigger dreams. Donald went to Tech on a basketball and academic scholarship, and she went to Chicago on a music scholarship."

"I thank God Brooks and I got back together. I can't imagine my life without him." She heard the baby fussing in the other room. "I guess it's time to feed Dallas."

Her mother hugged her and said, "I love happily ever after stories. I wish everyone could find true love like your dad and me and you and Brooks."

"What do you know about Sam Howard?"

Donna shrugged. "He was in our class. He was quiet, like he was always in his brother's shadow. The county covers miles and miles of Texas, and I didn't know him or his wife."

After settling in the rocking chair with her baby, Katie said, "Winn's mom is cute and seems nice."

Her mother laughed. "Andrea looked like she'd swallowed a cow when I introduced them."

Katie joined in the laughter. "I can't wait to see how this plays out."

***

When Faith Timberman returned home, Winn asked her about church. "It's different than any church I've ever attended. Not fancy like the first church Sam goes to. They meet in a metal building that looks like a barn. People wear jeans, boots, and cowboy hats. The band plays country gospel music." She smoothed her hair behind her ear. "Did you know Brooks Travis, who sang with Canada Jones, sings in their band?"

"I heard that."

"They have children's church. I think Charity would enjoy that."

"Not yet, Mom. If your relationship works out with Sam, and you think you'll keep going to the church, maybe she can go with you later."

"I wish I had taken you to church when you were younger."

"You did some." He crossed his arms. "I didn't fit in with the first church crowd."

"You would fit in with the cowboys at this church. I really think you and Charity would like it." She went on to tell him about meeting Sam's old school friends, and how friendly everyone was, how they all said they hoped she and Sam would come back.

Winn wondered what would happen when she met Andrea, or rather, how Andrea would react knowing she was his mother.

Chapter Fifteen

Andrea advertised for a receptionist. With all the expenses of rebuilding, she couldn't afford to pay the salary for a licensed vet tech, but she could hire someone with office skills and train her to help with the animals. Going through the online applications, Chloe Jones seemed like the best candidate. Andrea liked her immediately during the interview. She had almost decided to give Chloe the job until she started talking about her family. Her husband Keith was a lineman for the county co-op. Could he be Winn's friend?

"Do you have any children?"

"Yes, I have a four-year old named Cassie, and a six-year-old named Caiden." She shared a few funny stories. Andrea tried to smile, but her face felt wooden. "My mother loves spending time with them, so childcare won't be a problem."

Andrea nodded. "I have a few more applicants to interview, and I'll get back with you."

Chloe pumped Andrea's hand. "I really would love to have this job. I'm a fast learner. I love meeting people, I love animals, and I'm ready for a change."

Oh the joys of small towns. Everybody knows somebody who knows somebody, if they don't know everybody.

Andrea looked through the applications again. Spelling errors, grammatical errors, no stable work experience. She needed help, someone she could trust and depend on. Chloe's cheerful disposition would be a delightful addition to the office. But . . . her husband works with Winn.

***

In the counselor's office she shared the positive things she had written in her notebook.

"How does that make you feel when you read about all the good choices you've made?" he asked.

She shrugged. "I feel pretty good just looking at the positive things, but as my Abuelo says, 'No matter how thin you slice the bread, it always has two sides.'"

"Let's talk about the other side." He steepled his fingers. "What is the very worst mistake you have made?"

She waved her hands in front of her. "Going to that club with Hunter."

He nodded. "What did you learn from that?"

"I learned not to trust men."

"Can you trust the men in your family?"

"Of course."

"Have they ever hurt you? Abused you in any way?"

Andrea leapt out of the chair. "I know you deal with crazies all the time, but nobody in my family is crazy or perverted or even mean!" She paced in front of his desk while he looked at her, his face

145

devoid of emotion. She sat down and said, "I'm sorry I exploded. I won't allow anyone to badmouth my family."

"Has that been a problem in the past? People badmouthing your family?"

She sighed deeply. She explained that the Cordovas were Spanish, land grant heirs in New Mexico. Attending school in West Texas, she was labeled a Mexican, as if it were something inferior. She had a boyfriend in middle school, but in high school, he told her his parents wouldn't let him date her because she wasn't "white." Perhaps that made her defensive, but she had always had a quick temper.

"Have you ever attended anger management classes?"

"I'm not that bad."

He raised his eyebrows. "Can you control your anger?"

"Most of the time."

"Would you like to attend an anger management group?"

She shook her head vigorously.

He opened a drawer and pulled out several pamphlets. "Take these and read them." He handed them to her and held out his hand. "May I see your notebook?"

He wrote something on it and gave it back to her. "This week, I would like you to write down the times you lost your temper. What triggered it? How did you react? What could you have done differently." He sat in his chair waiting for a response.

"The other side of the bread?"

146

"Yes."

She laughed. "I'm afraid this notebook isn't thick enough."

"Just the major blow ups, not every little annoyance."

"This week won't be as enjoyable." She rubbed her hands down her thighs.

"We have to deal with the tough stuff to make room for the good stuff. We have to empty our emotional cup." He opened his desk drawer and pulled out his prescription pad. "Have you had any more nightmares?"

"No, those pills knocked me out cold."

"I can write another prescription for this week, perhaps something milder."

"No, I don't want any more pills."

"Then I'll see you in two weeks."

***

On the drive back to her clinic, Andrea thought about her temper. Her dad used to call her his little spitfire. She may look like her mother and Abuelo, but her temperament came from her dad and Gramps. Brooks inherited the Cordova looks, musical ability, and temperament. Celina looked more like their dad, but she was quiet, calm, and patient like their mother and Abuelo.

She thought about Katie. They were best friends from the first grade until they went their separate ways in college. Katie was feisty, but her temper couldn't compare to Andrea's. All those years they never fought. It was the two of them against the world, actually three against the world counting Brooks. Celina, only a few years older, always acted more mature than the three of them put together. She was independent, serious, hard-working, a champion barrel racer, and rodeo queen. She had treated Andrea like a baby, just because she was the baby of the family. *Maybe I should to try to nurture a relationship with my sister.*

Andrea desperately needed help at the clinic. For the salary she could pay, the distance was too far for someone to drive from Lubbock every day. With limited applicants to choose from, she decided to offer Chloe the job. Winn probably wouldn't find out, but so what if he did?

***

Reading the pamphlets about anger, Andrea acknowledged that although she often felt irritation and annoyance, rage was rare. In first grade, she felt rage when older boys picked on Brooks and called him a little Mexican. She and Katie jumped in kicking, hitting, and scratching. Yes, she felt rage then because of the unprovoked harassment. Looking back, there was nothing she would do differently.

In third grade, Sonja Stringer stole candy from the teacher's desk and blamed it on Andrea. Even though she told the truth, the teacher didn't believe it. Andrea had to go to the principal's office, where she got five licks with the paddle. At recess, she grabbed Sonja by her stringy hair, knocked her on the ground, and kicked dirt in her face. The teacher dragged her back to the principal's office. She received five more licks and lost recess for a week. The trigger? Injustice and humiliation. She shouldn't have fought. Not only did she get in trouble at school, but her mother grounded her, so she couldn't ride her horse or play with Katie for a week.

In seventh grade, her math teacher made an error working a problem on the board. When Andrea corrected her, the teacher yelled at her and called her a trouble maker. Andrea told her at least she knew the right answer. She found herself once again in the principal's office. She explained the problem and worked the equation. The principal laughed and told her not to correct the teacher in front of the class, yet she still had to apologize to the teacher for being rude. The trigger? The injustice of being called a trouble maker when she was just trying to be helpful. The teacher started marking her correct answers wrong. Gramps was a math whiz. She showed him her papers, and he wrote notes to the teacher explaining how to work the problems to get the right answer. The teacher started picking on her for every move she made. Once she even kept her after class for "rolling her eyes." She talked to Gramps about it, and he talked to the principal. The teacher didn't yell at her after that, and the next year she was no longer at their school. The lesson from that experience is to respect authority, and when there is a problem, enlist help from another authority figure.

In high school, a boy grabbed her inappropriately when she walked down the aisle on the bus. She slapped his face and kneed him in the crotch. The trigger? Harassment. Brooks pulled her off of the guy and told him not to ever touch his sister again. She was banned from riding the bus for three weeks. If she hadn't attacked the guy, maybe *he* would have been kicked off the bus instead of her. She should have learned to control her temper and talk to the proper authorities.

In college, when Katie broke up with Brooks and said she was pregnant with some other guy's baby, the hurt turned to seething fury. After she cried until she could cry no more, Andrea wrote Katie a hate letter calling her dirty names and telling her she never wanted to see or talk to her again. As time went by, the anger smoldered to bitterness. Andrea built a wall and refused to let anyone get in. What should she have done differently? Try to talk to Katie, try to understand her point of view, support her and be her friend.

In vet school, Hunter provoked her to rage. After the drugging disaster, she confronted him, he laughed and told her good luck trying to prove anything. His family made big donations to the school. Nothing would happen to him. Andrea kept it all in until she couldn't cope with the nightmares. During counseling, she began working out more. She earned her black belt. Each time she sparred, she imagined Hunter's face. She became so aggressive her instructor told her if she couldn't control herself while sparring, he would ban her from the club. The trigger? Harassment, frustration, hurt, and injustice. What should she have done differently? She should have filed a complaint. She didn't, so now she needed to let it go.

Andrea read through the anger pamphlets. She realized she

was easily annoyed, stemming from her impatience and her perfectionist tendencies. *I am strong. I can control my anger.*

Think before you speak. How many times had her mother told her to count to ten before she opened her mouth, not to say anything until she was calm? The problem is that sometimes counting to ten wasn't enough for her to get calm.

Physical activity reduces stress and anger. Karate helped her work off her frustrations. Her yoga and breathing exercises helped her relax. She didn't do the meditation stuff, but maybe she should start meditating on scripture and listening to inspirational music while doing yoga.

Pause and focus on solutions instead of problems. She was a great problem solver academically and in life. Not so much with relationships. She needed to make a plan to completely restore her relationship with Katie. That will require complete forgiveness. She could do that. She could reach out to her sister Celina and build a relationship. Winn? The solution is not to see him again. Well, she may see him around, but she didn't have to *see him* see him.

Don't hold a grudge. Brooks once told her she was the queen of grudges. Forgiveness didn't come easy to her. She read somewhere that holding a grudge is like taking poison and expecting the other person to die. She could forgive Katie, but could she forgive Winn? He lied to her. Well, he didn't exactly lie. He just didn't tell her the whole truth, which is just as bad. But she hadn't told her family what happened with Hunter. She couldn't. She didn't want to hurt them.

They would want to hurt Hunter, which could get them into a lot of trouble. She could *never* forgive Hunter.

Use humor to release tension. Winn does that. She loves his sense of humor. Laughter is good medicine for the soul.

Know when to seek help. I'm going to a counselor. I don't know the preacher well enough to talk to him. *God, I know You. Can You help me?*

She remembered some of the scriptures she had memorized when she was in youth group and wrote them on index cards to put on her mirror and in her pocket:

"I can do all things through Christ who strengthens me." – Philippians 4:13

"My grace is sufficient for you, for My power is made perfect in weakness." –II Corinthians 12:9

Chapter Sixteen

Keith came into work whistling. "Guess what?"

"You won the lottery?" Winn asked.

Keith laughed. "Maybe a small jackpot stretched over many years."

Winn concentrated on his work orders for the day. Keith shoulder butted him and said, "Aren't you even kind of curious?"

"If you want to tell me something, just spit it out."

Keith's grin spread from ear to ear. "Chloe got a job. She wanted to do more than work at the preschool part-time."

Winn nodded. "If you're happy, I'm happy."

"You wanna' know where she's working?" Winn shrugged, so Keith continued. "She's working for the girl vet, Dr. Travis."

"Does Chloe know I kind of dated Andrea?"

"I haven't told her." He laughed. "Chloe told her I'm a lineman. I wonder how long it will take the vet to put two and two together."

"When she does, Chloe may be out the door." Winn's brow wrinkled. "I hope she doesn't lose her job because of me."

As he went through his daily tasks, Winn couldn't get Andrea out of his mind. He really liked her. Maybe he loved her. He thought about dropping by her clinic but decided against it. He had been praying more lately than he had in a long time, maybe ever. He asked God to work it out if they were meant to be together.

***

At his appointment with the counselor, he talked about the anger he harbored against Janae for driving while under the influence. The accident that took her life could have hurt or killed Charity, too. Actually it had hurt his little girl because she had to grow up without a mother. "Whenever I get mad about it, I pray and thank God that I still have Charity, that she wasn't injured."

The counselor steepled his fingers and asked, "Have you ever considered remarrying?"

"No, I've tried to focus on my daughter. I want to be there for her more than my dad was for me." Then he told the counselor about Andrea. "I can imagine myself spending the rest of my life with her. But, of course, that's not going to happen."

"Have you done everything you can to make amends?"

"I tried, but she blocked my number so I can't even call her." He laughed. "I've thought about stopping by to see her, but I don't want her to accuse me of harassing or stalking her."

The counselor nodded. "So you're ready to put her out of your mind and move on?"

"That's easier said than done."

"Things like this take time to accept." The counselor stood. "You seem to be coping with your anger issues well. Why don't we schedule a follow-up appointment in a month?"

"You think I need to come back?" Winn shrugged. "I feel better already."

"That's entirely up to you. I wish all my clients were as well adjusted as you."

Winn shook his hand. "Thanks for everything." He paused at the door. "I saw Andrea in your office the first time I came. I don't know why she's so angry and uptight, but I hope you can help her."

The counselor nodded. "I'll do my best."

As Winn drove home, he wondered if he had really done all he could. He slowed down as he approached Andrea's clinic. It was after closing time. No vehicles were in front, and he couldn't see if her pickup was parked in the back. No, he wouldn't go to her clinic. *God what should I do?*

***

The next morning Keith sauntered into work. "Chloe loves her job. All night she talked about how great Dr. Travis is, how gentle and patient she is with animals and kids."

Winn crossed his arms on his chest. "I just hope Andrea doesn't turn on her."

"In case you haven't noticed, Chloe is charming, all sunshine and smiles. Everybody loves her." Keith winked.

Winn held his hands out, palms up. "What? You don't think I'm charming?"

"That's not exactly the word I would use to describe you."

Keith laughed. "Did you know Brooks Travis, the singer, is Andrea's brother?"

"Yes. He was one of the men who came to Andrea's aid at the Fourth of July Street dance." He shook his head. "Not that she needed any help. I was the one lying in the dirt on my backside."

"Yeah, the men in her family look pretty tough. Her dad is Dustin Travis, the champion roper."

After comparing work orders for the day, Winn headed toward the door. "Stay cool."

"Another thing—Dr. Travis invited us to the cowboy church Sunday."

Winn stopped dead in his tracks. "Are you going?"

"Chloe wants to go. We've never been in church much, but she wants to take the kids." Keith raised his eyebrows. "She can be very persuasive and always gets her way."

"My mom and Sam Howard went last week."

"So how's that working out?"

Winn shrugged. "They like the church." He shifted from one foot to the other. "They met Brooks and his family. I'm wondering what will happen if she meets Andrea."

"Does your mom know about Andrea, the lady wrestler?"

"She's not a wrestler." Winn made Karate chops with his hands. "She's into some kind of martial arts. I think Karate." He straightened his posture. "My mom knows a little about it but not her name."

Keith laughed. "How are things going with Mr. Howard and your mom?"

"She likes him—a lot." He shuffled his feet. "I just hope she doesn't get hurt."

"Mr. Howard seems like an okay guy, and your mom is smart, sweet, and attractive."

Winn turned. "I'll see you later." Looking back over his shoulder, he said, "And don't be looking at my mom."

As he drove along the highway, the deep blue Texas sky reminded him of Andrea's beautiful eyes. Every song on the classic country station reminded him of her and her love for music. The hot Texas sun reminded him how much she lit up his life. The endless miles of nothing reminded him how empty he felt without her.

Chapter Seventeen

Sunday morning the preacher at the cowboy church preached about anger. He used an illustration about a bull at the rodeo. The chute opened, that bull was so angry and intent on hurting the rider he'd thrown off that he rammed his head into the metal railing and broke his neck.

Then the preacher brought in the practical application. He said, "God is emotional. Psalm 7:11 says He gets angry every day. God made us emotional beings capable of anger. Ephesians 4:26 tells us it's okay to get angry, but don't let your anger control you. Don't stay mad. Forgive, get over it, and get on with life."

Andrea bowed her head and prayed: *Okay, first the counselor and now the preacher. Lord, I know I have let my anger control me. Please forgive me, and help me forgive Katie and Winn. I can never forgive Hunter. What he did was unforgivable. Thank You that I never have to see him again.*

After church, Andrea met her family at the back where Brooks stood with the band. Chloe and Keith walked up. Chloe said, "Dr. Travis, this is my husband Keith. Keith, this is Dr. Andrea Travis."

Keith smiled and extended his hand. "I've heard a lot about you."

She hesitated before nodding and shaking his hand. "I'm happy to have Chloe working in my office. She has already been a great help."

Sam Howard joined the group. Keith introduced Chloe to his boss and said, "This is Mrs. Timberman, Winn's mother."

Andrea stared at the petite woman. Her hair was the same blondish brown as Winn's. Her eyes were the same cloudy blue-gray, surrounded by smile crinkles. Faith caught her staring, so Andrea looked away.

Keith said, "Have you met Dr. Travis? Chloe just started working in her veterinary clinic."

"I met so many people last week, but I do remember meeting you. You and your mother have the most beautiful, deep blue eyes," Faith smiled at her, just like Winn's light-up-your-life smile.

Andrea looked around, searching for Winn hiding in the crowd. "It's nice to meet you, again." She could feel the blush flooding her cheeks. Austin ran up and hugged her, giving her a chance to look away.

He saw Keith's son and said, "This is my new friend Caiden."

"I'll see you all in a little while," Andrea said and hurried out the door.

As she drove to the ranch, she wondered what was being said at church. Would her parents, Brooks, or Katie tell Mrs. Timberman they knew Winn or that they had met him? Had Winn told his mother about her?

159

She went straight to the barn and saddled her favorite palomino. Maybe the wind in her face from a fast ride would clear her thoughts and emotions. As the horse ran through the pasture, she thought about Winn. She didn't want to see him again, but his friend's wife was now working in her clinic. His boss and his mother were attending her church.

God, can I forgive him without talking to him? Do I need to tell him I'm sorry for flipping him on the ground and calling him a liar? Lord, can I just tell you I'm sorry and leave it at that?

She thought about the other things the preacher said in his message. We're supposed to forgive as God forgave us. If we have something against someone, we're supposed to go to them and work it out. We're supposed to do our part to get along.

Okay, Lord. Help me talk to Katie first. One step at a time.

***

After her ride, she called Katie and asked if they could talk, privately.

Katie met her at the door. "Brooks took Austin for an ice cream at Pat's. Then they're going to the ranch so your dad can help Austin with his roping." She poured two glasses of fresh-squeezed lemonade. "You want to sit at the table or in the living room?"

"Let's sit at the table." Andrea took a drink and rubbed at the condensation on her glass.

Katie handed Andrea a coaster. "So, was that a bit awkward meeting Winn's mom, his boss, and his coworker?"

Andrea shrugged. "His mom is cute."

Katie raised her eyebrows. "She looks a lot like Winn."

Andrea took another drink and licked her lips. "I didn't come here to talk about Winn."

Katie's downcast eyes showed her discomfort. "Okay. We can talk about anything you want."

"Well, you heard the preacher's message today about anger and forgiveness." Katie nodded, so Andrea continued. "I was so angry when you said you were pregnant and some guy in Chicago was the dad." Katie opened her mouth, but Andrea raised her hand. "I was angry because I loved you, like a sister, actually more than my own sister. I always imagined us being together, the Three Amigos. It shattered my dream. It broke my heart. It broke Brooks's heart, which made me angry."

Andrea looked around the pristine red and white kitchen. "Our friendship was pure, built on trust. When I love, I love deeply, completely. The fire in my veins can turn to anger and hate, and my love for you turned to hatred. It smoldered into bitterness." She wiped the tears from her eyes. "I'm sorry about the letter I wrote you. I'm sorry for the way I treated you when you came home."

Katie reached across the table and patted her hand. "It's okay. Even though I thought it was the best thing to do at the time, I did lie."

"No, it's not okay. My behavior was inexcusable. Will you please forgive me?"

Katie stood and hugged her friend. "I forgive you. Will you forgive me?"

"Yes." Andrea sobbed as they held each other. When she regained her composure, she pulled away and blew her nose. "I've been going to a counselor in Lubbock. For my anger."

Katie sat back in her chair and nodded. "I probably should have gone to a counselor. Maybe I would have handled things differently. I blamed Brooks for things that were not his fault, and I let my anger turn to bitterness, also."

"If I tell you something, do you promise not to tell anyone, not even Brooks?"

"I promise."

Andrea sucked in a breath. "You know I didn't date much in high school." She frowned. "The pickings were pretty slim."

"You can say that for sure." Katie listed some of the jerks they had known in school.

"I didn't date much in college. Besides studying to keep my scholarship, I had some trust issues."

"I'm sorry."

"It's not your fault." Andrea shook her head. "I didn't date much in vet school, either."

"I always figured you'd marry a vet."

"I guess I did, too. I knew I didn't want to marry someone who rode the rodeo circuit like my dad." She clasped and unclasped her hands. "Anyway, I did meet a guy in vet school. He was good-looking, charming, smart—we became lab partners." She rubbed her hands over her forehead and pinched her nose. She hung her head as her jaw tightened. She told Katie about Hunter, the date rape drug, the nightmares.

"So nobody knows?"

"You and the counselor."

"I am so very sorry."

"Me, too. It did a number on me, but I'm doing better now." She wiped the tears from her eyes and looked up. "When we were best friends, we told each other everything."

"I'm sorry I wasn't there for you when that happened."

"I'm sorry I wasn't there for you, either." Andrea shook her head. "I didn't tell my family about Hunter, because I was afraid they would react and want to hurt him since the legal system wouldn't punish him."

"Is it too late to press charges now?"

"Since I didn't see a doctor or have a blood test, I couldn't prove anything." She finished her lemonade. "The past is over and done. I want to move on."

Katie nodded. "So, moving back to the present—the man Winn's mom is dating is the brother to my Aunt LeAnn's one and only love."

"Her one and only, huh?"

"Definitely." She told Andrea some of the things her aunt had said and how it helped her make the decision to give up the dream of

163

symphony to come back home and marry Brooks, the love of her life.

"Do you think there's just one love for everyone?"

"No. I think there's a best love for everyone. But just like everything else in life, when we mess up, God is always willing to give us another chance, a fresh start. He's always ready to forgive. His mercies are new every morning."

Andrea nodded. "You know Winn was married before and has a little girl?"

"Yes, but his wife is dead." She raised her eyebrows. "Winn, on the other hand, is young and very much alive."

"I don't see anything happening there."

Katie picked up the pitcher of lemonade. "Would you like another glass?"

Andrea nodded. "I do need to forgive Winn for lying."

"Did he lie?" Katie raised her eyebrows.

"Not telling the whole truth is the same as lying."

"Would you like a cookie? Your mom sent some snickerdoodles home for Austin?"

Andrea shook her head. "Winn loved my mom's cookies. He likes blizzards, too."

"If this is true confession time, how much do you like the guy?"

Andrea made designs on the condensation of her glass. "I liked him a lot. More than any guy I've ever known." She licked her lips. "I felt things with him that I've never felt for anyone else."

164

"So when are you going to tell him you forgive him?"

"I've told God I forgive him. Do you think that's enough?"

"Seriously?" Katie giggled. "No, you need to tell him, for your sake and his."

"I need to pray about it."

"Why do you need to pray about doing something when you know it's the right thing to do?"

Chapter Eighteen

Sunday evening after putting Charity to bed, Faith and Winn sat on the back porch drinking iced tea. Faith said, "Next week, I would like to take Charity to the cowboy church. She knows Chloe and Cassie from preschool. They were at church with Keith and Caiden, of course." She sipped her tea. "I would like you to come with us. I think you would like it."

"What do you think I would like?"

"The casual atmosphere. The country gospel music. The preacher is straight forward, not showy. The people are friendly."

Winn raised his eyebrows. "So you've met some nice people?"

"Sam met an old friend he went to school with, Richard Kane. His son-in-law is Brooks Travis, who was a back-up singer for Canada Jones. Brooks has a very pretty sister, a vet who just hired Chloe to work for her." She winked. "You already know people there, with the possibility of meeting new friends."

"New friends, huh?"

She grinned. "Yes, and I really want you to get to know Sam on a personal level."

"You can take Charity, but I think I'll pass." He poured out the ice, walked in the kitchen, and put his glass in the dishwasher. "Good night."

But it wasn't a good night for Winn. He couldn't get Andrea out of his mind. His mother thought she was pretty—well, who wouldn't? But his mother might already have a negative opinion of her. If his mother married Sam Howard, would they want to live at the ranch? He couldn't live with his mother and another man. If his mom married and moved out, where would that leave him and Charity? It would be hard taking care of her by himself while working full time, being on call, and taking care of the ranch. Whatever other problems Andrea had, at least she had a support system with her extended family. He wished he had siblings. He wished he had known grandparents who loved him. He wanted that for Charity. She hated visiting Janae's parents because she said they weren't fun and didn't let her play.

Winn dreamed about Andrea and him together, with Charity and a little dark-haired boy, sitting beneath the big oak tree at the back of his house. Only in the dream, it was their house. The sun formed a halo around Andrea's head, the bright gold contrasting with her black hair. As the sun began to set, the image of Andrea floated away. He reached to pull her back, but she slipped away, his dream angel soared up to heaven, leaving him alone and empty.

He awoke clutching his pillow, drenched in perspiration. Throwing back the covers, he slipped on his jeans and walked out on the back porch. Trillions of stars sparkled against the inky, black sky.

The full moon illuminated his property, casting spooky shadows across the pasture. Coyotes howled—too close for comfort. Then he heard Clyde's distinct bark followed by growls and howls.

"Clyde, come home." He yelled and whistled as he turned and rushed back into the house. He slipped on his socks and boots, grabbed the shotgun, and ran back outside. He jumped on the John Deere Gator and headed toward the ruckus. His heart sank as he saw two coyotes attacking Clyde. He shot one before the other ran away. Shooting into the shadows, he heard the coyote yelp in the distance. Looking at his Catahoula-heeler cross, he saw a tangled mass of blood and fur. Picking him up and placing him in the back of the Gator, he sped to the house.

"Stay, Clyde," he said patting the dog on the head. Winn rushed inside and called Andrea on the house phone. "Please don't hang up on me. My dog was attacked by coyotes. Will you treat him if I bring him in?"

"Yes." She took a deep breath. "Be careful and don't get any blood on you."

Looking down at his hands, he said, "A little late for that."

"Scrub it off right now. If you have any open wounds or cuts, scrub them for at least five minutes. Change clothes and put them in a plastic trash bag where your little girl can't touch them." She softened her voice. "Winn, I'll be ready when you get here."

Winn opened the cabinet door and pulled out a trash bag and disinfectant wipes. He washed everything he had touched, stepped out on the porch, stripped off his clothes and boots, dropped them in the trash bag and slung it away from the porch. He ran to his shower and scrubbed from head to toe, thankful he didn't have any cuts or abrasions. He dressed quickly in old jeans and rubber boots, grabbed old towels from the cleaning closet, and headed back outside.

Clyde whined as Winn wrapped him in the towels and laid him in the floorboard of his truck. Driving to Andrea's clinic, he told Clyde what a brave dog he was for protecting the ranch from the scroungy predators. The dog moaned. "Andrea will fix you up, and you'll be good as new."

When he arrived at the clinic, Andrea met him at the door and led him to the operating room. "Put him on the table," she said through her surgical mask. With gloved hands, she gave the dog a sedative and began to wash him. "He's lost a lot of blood, but if he doesn't have any serious internal injuries, he should be okay." After shaving his fur, she asked "Did the coyotes get away?"

"One is dead for sure. The other one yelped, so I at least clipped it."

"How many were there?"

"Two." Winn rubbed his hand over his face. "Clyde is fearless, but he's no match for two big coyotes."

Andrea started an IV of antibiotics. "His wounds are superficial. I'll insert tubes so the infection can drain."

"So you can patch him up and he'll be okay?"

Seeing the pain in his eyes, she focused on cleaning and

sewing up the dog.

"He'll be okay, right?"

Andrea looked into his stormy gray eyes and averted her gaze. Clearing her throat she said, "There's always a chance of rabies."

"Clyde's had all his shots."

"That's good." She nodded. "Go over there and scrub up. Take your t-shirt off and drop it in the trash can. Put on that lab coat."

"Yes, ma'am." He flashed her that mouth-watering smile, and she felt the blush creep up her neck.

Once Clyde was in a kennel, Andrea disposed of her surgical clothes and sterilized the operating room. Glancing at the clock, she said, "It's almost four. What time do you usually get up?"

"I usually get up around five so I can take care of the stock before I get ready for work." He shifted from foot to foot.

"Would you like a cup of coffee or tea?"

He nodded. "Coffee sounds good."

She led him to her break room/kitchen and showed him the Keurig carrousel. "What would you like?" His smile warmed her more than any cup of coffee ever could.

He twirled the carrousel. "I don't know much about fancy flavored coffee."

She picked up a pod. "This is plain old fashioned brew. You want it?"

"Okay."

Her hands shook as she put it in the machine and placed a mug

170

in the holder. She took his hands in hers turning them to examine them, inspecting his cuticles, surveying his arms. "Your hands and arms are clear. Do you have any open wounds anywhere on your body?"

He smiled mischievously. "I don't think so, but you can look."

"This is serious. The sheriff's department will have to pick up the coyotes and take them to Lubbock for testing. If they have rabies, you will have to have shots."

He grimaced. "In the stomach?"

"No, the modern cell-based vaccines are similar to flu shots. You would receive immunoglobulin followed by four doses of rabies vaccine."

She made herself a cup of herbal tea. Placing the mugs on the table, she pulled out a chair and waved for him to sit across from her. She took a sip of tea and cleared her throat. "I'm sorry I flipped you on the ground at the street dance."

"I understand you were mad and had a right to be."

She shook her head. "I was mad, but I didn't have a right to do what I did." Taking a sip of tea she said, "You didn't exactly lie to me, so I shouldn't have called you a liar."

"I should have told you about Charity—after I got to know you." His eyes looked like a wounded puppy. "I wanted to tell you, but I didn't know how." He swallowed hard and lowered his voice. "I was afraid I'd lose you before we even had a chance to develop a relationship."

She pinched the bridge of her nose. "I'm sorry for what I did and said, but I'm not ready for a relationship."

He nodded. "Friends?"

She shook her head. "I have some things I need to work through."

"I'm sorry you've been hurt." His gray eyes clouded. "I would never intentionally do anything to hurt you."

"Thanks." She stood and put her mug in the sink. "If you're going to get started on your chores by five, you better get going."

He stepped to the sink and rinsed his mug, his arm brushing hers. He unbuttoned the lab coat.

"You can wear it home and bring it back when you come to get Clyde."

"I don't need it." He removed it and handed it to her.

The blood cursed through her veins as her eyes roved from his biceps to his pectoral muscles to his taut abs. She hoped he couldn't hear her heartbeat.

"Do you see any open wounds?" He turned around so she could view his back.

"What?" *Get a grip, Andrea.* "No, I don't see any problems." *No, there's definitely nothing wrong with his body.*

"When can I get Clyde?"

"Um, call when you get off work and we'll see how he's doing. Maybe you should stay home and show the sheriff where the coyotes are." She walked to the desk and picked up a pen and notepad. "Give me your address so I can report it to the sheriff's department."

After he left, she buried her face in the lab coat and inhaled his fresh, clean, manly scent. She showered, sniffed the lab coat again, put it on over her clothes, and wistfully imagined being close to Winn.

***

His mother was cooking breakfast when he walked into the house. She raised her eyebrows when she saw his shirtless torso and the rubber boots.

"Good morning," he said as he walked through the kitchen.

"Wait just a minute." She turned from the stove and waved the spatula at him. "What're you doing?"

"Let me take a shower real quick. Then I'll explain." As the hot water pulsated on his skin, he prayed that the coyotes didn't have rabies, that he would be okay, that Clyde would be okay, that Andrea would be okay, that she would get over whatever had hurt her.

After he dressed, he walked into the kitchen and relayed the night's events to his mother.

"Why did you take Clyde to the new vet? We've always used Westridge in town."

He took a gulp of coffee. "Well, Keith's wife Chloe likes her and talks about how good and patient she is."

She nodded. "Uh huh, I see."

No you don't. He kissed his mother on the cheek. "Gotta run." From the look on her face, she saw more than he was willing to say. The sheriff's animal control vehicle pulled into the drive. They found and bagged the first coyote and the second one, a female, not far away.

Driving to work, Winn couldn't wait till quitting time so he could see Andrea again, and Clyde, of course.

***

When Chloe arrived at work, Andrea explained about Clyde and how to take care of him when she had to go out on a call.

Looking at the chart, Chloe said, "Winn Timberman works with my husband Keith. He's a great guy, fun, a good worker. His little girl is in the same preschool as Cassie, where I worked part time."

"How well do you know him?"

"He's probably Keith's best friend at work. He's been to the house for dinner, so the girls could have a playdate. The co-op has lots of family functions, so I know him that way. I've never seen him drink or heard him curse." Chloe set aside the chart. "I wonder why he didn't take his dog to Westridge Veterinary since it's closer to his ranch."

Andrea shrugged. "Do you need anything else before I leave?"

"Is there something special I need to do today?"

"Just be here in case anyone comes in." Andrea handed her a book. "This will be good to help you decide if you want to pursue

174

your vet tech certificate online. In fact, it probably covers most of what would be in your first course."

"Thanks. Have a good day."

"I should be back before lunch."

***

At five o'clock Winn called Andrea. "Hey, how's Clyde?"

"He's doing well, but I need to keep him at least one more night. We may have to keep him quarantined if the coyotes test positive for rabies even though he's had his shot."

"Oh, okay." His voice dripped with disappointment.

"You can come see him if you want to. It might make him feel better."

"It would make me feel better."

She could hear the smile in his voice. "I'm locking up for the day. Just ring the bell, and I'll let you in."

The mirror reflected dark circles under her eyes, betraying her lack of sleep. She didn't have time to shower, so she washed her face, applied fresh makeup, brushed her hair, and put on a clean tank top.

She walked to Clyde's kennel and asked him how he felt. "Do you miss your daddy? He's coming to see you. Will that make you happy?" His tail thumped. "It makes me happy to see dogs happy, reunited with owners who love them."

The buzzer rang, and Andrea jumped. "Are you ready, Clyde?" On the way to the door, she stopped and checked her reflection in the mirror. She applied a second coat of lip gloss and

175

licked her lips. The buzzer sounded again. She opened the door and said, "Are you a bit impatient?"

He looked at her lips, her tank top, her jeans. He gazed into her eyes and blushed as he said, "I was afraid you didn't hear me."

She closed and locked the door. *Wow, that's an improvement. Inside alone with the door locked and no fear or anxiety.* "Come on back. Clyde is doing well, but I think it would be best to keep him tonight so I can give him pain meds, which will help keep him calm and quiet. You should be able to take him home tomorrow."

"Hey, Clyde, old buddy." Winn knelt and rubbed his dog behind the ears.

His gentleness with the dog spoke volumes about him. Chloe spoke highly of him. *Maybe he's okay. Well, more than okay.* He kept talking to the dog, loving on him. When he stood to go, the dog struggled to stand. "He's still groggy, but tomorrow he'll be good to go."

"It's okay, Clyde. The nice lady will take good care of you. I'll be back tomorrow to get you." As he walked away, the dog whimpered. The pain on Winn's face tugged at Andrea's heart more than the whining of the dog.

In the lobby, Winn asked, "Can I buy you dinner or something to repay you for getting up in the middle of the night to take care of my dog?"

"No need. The bill will more than repay me." Andrea giggled. "Besides, I have my yogurt, apple, and salad." She touched her flat tummy. "I need to eat light, so I can enjoy my mom's home cooking on Sundays."

He looked at her hand resting on her snug jeans, his eyes moving up to her lips. "Well, okay. I'll see you tomorrow."

After she closed and locked the door, she wondered what it would be like to kiss him, when she was ready, which wasn't now.

***

At the dinner table, Faith asked Winn about Clyde. He finished chewing his chicken and guzzled his tea. "Andrea thinks it would be best to keep him one more night."

Her eyebrows arched in overdrive. "Andrea, huh?"

"Dr. Travis." He felt perspiration bead up on his forehead.

"I think her mother's name is Caramel, like the candy lady."

"The candy lady?" Charity clapped her hands. "Did you bring me some cookies from the candy lady?"

"Sorry. I haven't seen the candy lady."

"Just her daughter? Dr. Travis?"

He looked at the frown on his mother's face. Would she play the victim? The Nazi controller?

"I like her cookies," Charity said.

"Don't chew with your mouth full," Faith chided her granddaughter.

The little girl clouded up. "That's what my gram-mother says."

Winn dabbed at the tears in his daughter's eyes. "Gamma is

right, and so is your Grandmother Fontaine."

"I don't like Gram-mother Fontaine." Her little lip pouched out. "She says I don't know how to act like a lady."

Winn hugged her. "You are my princess, and a princess is more special than a lady."

"I made tapioca pudding for dessert." His mother smiled until she noticed Charity's turned up nose. "Would you like to make some brownies?" The little girl nodded. "Eat your dinner and we'll make brownies."

"Yumm," Winn rubbed his stomach. "Brownies and tapioca pudding." His mother's frown told him the discussion wasn't over.

After Charity was in bed, his mother asked him to sit on the back porch with her. "So, Dr. *Andrea* Travis is your friend."

"Actually, right now she is my vet. That's all."

"But you took Clyde to her instead of Westridge?"

"She's just starting her practice and can use the business." He sighed. "I like her even though there is no chance of a relationship."

"No chance?" Her mouth puckered.

"No chance." He stood and leaned on the porch rail. "Not now, anyway. Maybe never."

"I don't want to see you, or Charity, get hurt."

"I don't want to see you get hurt, either."

Her mouth dropped open. "Sam is a gentleman. We're both mature adults and know what we're doing."

"Look at me, Mom." He uncrossed his arms and waved them

178

in front of him. "I am an adult. I may not know what I'm doing, but I will protect Charity and make sure she doesn't get hurt."

"Guard your heart."

"You, too, Mom."

"Sam and I love each other. He has asked me to marry him."

"Kind of sudden isn't it?"

"I don't want to rush things, but I do want you to get to know him. If you won't go to church with us on Sunday, will you at least eat dinner with us?"

"I'll eat dinner with you, and Charity can go to church with you." He leaned over and kissed his mother on the cheek. "Goodnight."

Winn had trouble falling asleep. He thought about his mom and Sam Howard. He thought about him and Charity living alone. Mostly he thought about Andrea. Could they ever have a relationship? His mom said she knew she loved Sam. He thought he loved Andrea. He knew she had feelings for him. They definitely had chemistry. But he had a history that included a little girl. She had a history that kept her from trusting.

***

Tuesday Winn called Andrea's phone. Still blocked. He called the clinic and Chloe answered. "May I speak to Dr. Travis please?"

"She isn't in right now. May I take a message."

"This is Winn Timberman. I just wanted to talk to her about my dog Clyde."

179

"Hey, Winn. Clyde seems to be doing really well. I think Andrea, I mean Dr. Travis, said you can pick him up this afternoon. Would you like to have her cell phone number?"

"No thanks. Could you leave her a message and ask her to call me?"

"Sure thing. Have a good day and stay safe."

***

At four o'clock Winn's cell phone played "Waltz Across Texas." He smiled as he answered. "Hello, Dr. Travis."

She giggled. "You may call me Andrea."

"Okay. I tried to call, but my number is still blocked."

"The tests results came back, and the coyotes did not have rabies. You may come and get Clyde anytime."

"Great!" He sucked in air. "I'm going to stop by Dairy Queen on my way to the clinic. Since you have to eat, and I have to eat, I thought maybe we could eat together."

"That sounds good. I've worked up quite an appetite today."

"Would you like a Flamethrower Grill Burger to go with your Chocolate Xtreme Blizzard?"

"I think a small burger will be enough with a Blizzard."

"I'll see you around five."

"I'll be ready." She took a quick shower, donned clean jeans and a tank top, and applied fresh makeup. She sprayed on cologne to cover up any remaining horse smell.

***

Winn rang the buzzer on the door while balancing Dairy Queen bags and a drink tray. Looking at her damp hair, he said, "You're all fresh and clean, and I'm all dirty and sweaty."

"That's fine. I understand about hard work." Her smile melted his heart. "I can't smell anything but burgers and fries and," she sniffed, "onion rings?"

He laughed. "I promise I won't blow my onion breath on you."

She gave him a wicked wink. "But will you share?"

"Anything you want, you've got it." *Since you already have my heart.*

Andrea snitched several of his onion rings while he told her about an old man who knocked down the power pole in his pasture and was mad at the co-op because he had no power in his house. "You are so funny. How many voices can you imitate?"

"Ah, I am a man of mean-ni voiches. Vaht vould you like to hear, my dear?" *Did he just call her dear?* She stopped laughing.

"I guess we should finish eating so you can take Clyde home."

He nodded and took a slurp of his Blizzard. "You met my mom at the cowboy church."

"Yes." Her long lashes fluttered, sending shock waves through his body. "Does she know about the street dance?"

"I just told her you got mad because I didn't tell you about Charity." He paused. He started to reach for her hand but pulled back. "I didn't tell her your name." He laughed. "Or that you flipped

181

me on my behind."

"So she doesn't know it was me?"

"Well," *What should he say? The truth this time.* "She kind of figured it out when I brought Clyde here instead of Westridge." He took another drink of Blizzard. "She also met your mother."

"My mother?"

"Yes." He thought of her mother with the same beautiful blue eyes and black hair. "When I gave Charity the cookies your mother made, I told her they were from a friend's mother, who is named Carmella. It sounds like caramel, so she called her the candy lady."

She smiled. "The candy lady? My mother would like that." She swirled her Blizzard with a straw. "So your mother probably hates me."

"She doesn't hate you." He looked at her eyes, her lips. He definitely didn't hate her. "She thinks you're very pretty. She also wants to take Charity to the cowboy church. She thinks I would like it, too."

When she looked into his eyes, he wondered if she could see his true feelings. *His true feelings? He wasn't even sure what his true feelings were.*

"I like the cowboy church. I think you would like it, too."

"You wouldn't mind if I went?"

"Of course not. Remember, I invited you to go—before." She averted her gaze. "It's a big church. We might not even see each other."

182

"Yes, before. Would it make you uncomfortable if we saw each other at church, now?"

"Not as long as your mom doesn't hate me."

"She doesn't hate you." He wouldn't be able to keep his eyes off of her if he saw her at church. "I guess I better take Clyde home now."

Chapter Nineteen

The counselor asked Andrea to share her journal entries about anger. She told him about the pastor's message on anger and how she felt God was speaking directly to her. "So I talked with Katie and asked her to forgive me."

"How did that feel?"

"Really good, like part of my life was restored and the hole in my heart filled in." She took a deep breath and told him about Winn bringing Clyde to her clinic, about apologizing and telling him she is not ready for a relationship.

"How did that make you feel?"

"It made me feel like I'm not really a bad person."

"Did you think you were a bad person?"

She rubbed her hands down her jeans. "I have acted badly at times."

"Everyone behaves badly sometimes. That doesn't make someone a bad person."

"Thank you." She told the counselor about hiring Chloe, her husband's friendship with Winn, meeting Winn's mother at church. "So he may come to the church my family and I attend."

"How do you feel about that?"

"I invited him to church, before, when we were kind of friends, but he wouldn't come." She licked her lips. "I can't keep him from coming to church. I wouldn't try to stop anyone from worshipping God."

"Do you want to talk about Winn?"

"I thought you didn't discuss one client with another."

"I'm asking if you want to discuss your feelings for him."

She shook her head. "No. I mean, I don't know." She closed her eyes and exhaled. "I don't know what I feel." He sat patiently waiting. She felt tears pool in her eyes. "I can't trust myself."

He handed her a tissue. "This week I want you to record what you did right each day. If you make a mistake or lose your temper, write how you can make amends, and forgive yourself, immediately."

"What should I do about Winn?"

"You don't have to do anything about him." He steepled his fingers. "If he does something that makes you uncomfortable, then talk to him or tell someone else about it."

"What if just seeing him makes me uncomfortable?"

"In what way?"

She licked her lips. "I am attracted to him."

"Why does that make you uncomfortable?"

"Because." She pinched the bridge of her nose. "I feel things for him that I shouldn't feel."

"Physical attraction is normal and natural."

"I've never felt like this about anyone else." She fiddled with her fingers. "You know, I've never been close to a guy, like that. I'm mean, I've never . . . ."

"You mean you're a virgin?"

"In every sense of the word." She rubbed her palms down her jeans. "I've kissed a few guys, but that's it. Nothing else. Zilch."

He opened his desk drawer and handed her some pamphlets. "Read these. They will help you understand that you shouldn't be afraid of your feelings."

She could feel the blush creep up her neck and burn her cheeks. "I don't need those. I am a veterinarian. I fully understand animal urges and reproduction. What frightens me is the spiritual, emotional aspects." She plunked the pamphlets on his desk. "I will not become intimately involved with someone until I get married, and I'm certainly not ready for that." She paced in front of the desk. "I haven't even kissed the guy, yet I find myself thinking about it—a lot. And that scares me."

"Has he said or done anything inappropriate?"

"No! That's what's so crazy." She sat back down. "He hasn't done anything, made any kind of move, but I know he's attracted to me. I can feel it."

"And you don't like that?"

"No. I don't know." She whispered. "It makes me more attracted to him."

"Since you go to church and believe in God, perhaps you should pray about it. Ask God what you should do about your

186

thoughts and feelings. Keep your distance until you have a sense of whether you should pursue a relationship with Mr. Timberman or terminate all contact with him."

Andrea picked up her notebook, stood, and shook the counselor's hand. "Thank you."

"Do you want to come back next week, or do you want to wait a couple of weeks until you sort out your feelings."

"I'll make an appointment for a couple of weeks."

***

Andrea prayed as she drove. She asked God to help her think pure thoughts, to help clear her mind and give her discernment and direction. She stopped at Dairy Queen and ordered an Xtreme Chocolate Blizzard. *Yes, I need comfort food. My soul needs comfort.*

At the clinic, she ate her salad in silence. She thought about eating with Winn, him telling funny stories that made her laugh. She thought about meeting him in the tornado, how calm and strong he seemed. She thought about him helping her rebuild the clinic, about their one date to Lubbock. She thought about the street dance, laughing as he struggled to do the line dance. When they danced to "The Keeper of the Stars," Katie thought Winn was going to kiss her. She wanted him to, but she was afraid. She wanted him to kiss her the other night, but she was afraid. Was she afraid of him—or herself?

Before going to bed, Andrea read some verses about wisdom and discernment. She asked God to help her have an undivided mind. Long after she turned out the light she tossed and turned. Images of

Winn kept invading her mind, and she kept praying, "In all thy ways acknowledge Him, and He will direct thy paths." She fell asleep hugging her pillow. She dreamed of Winn laughing. She dreamed of them dancing at the street dance. They kissed and fireworks exploded. Night turned to day. She floated toward the gazebo at the Kane Ranch, decorated with red and white flowers for Brooks and Katie's wedding, only it wasn't their wedding. Winn stood at the gazebo waiting for her. Brooks sang "The Keeper of the Stars" as Abuelo played the guitar. Andrea looked into Winn's eyes and said, "I do."

She awoke with a start, her heart pounding. It had been so vivid, so real, not like a dream at all. The digital clock read 5:00. She thought about Winn getting up, feeding the stock, getting ready for work. She thought about how good he looked without a shirt. Shaking her head, she threw off the covers and got up. She prayed as she took a shower. "In all thy ways acknowledge Him, and He will direct thy paths."

She sat at the table in the break room and read her Bible as she ate yogurt and granola. When Chloe came to work, Andrea invited her to sit and have a cup of coffee. "Nothing's scheduled for the day, and we don't have any patients."

"Do you want me to go back home?"

"No. We could have three emergencies at once, which is why I need you."

Chloe fixed a mocha coffee. "Is there anything special you would like me to do today?"

"Just being here if I need you is enough." Andrea sipped her herbal tea. "While it's quiet tell me about your family. How did you and Keith meet?"

"I was going to Tech and working as a waitress. Keith came into the restaurant and something clicked. He kept coming in asking me out until I said yes. On the very first date, I knew he was the one for me."

"How did you know?"

"Besides being drop dead gorgeous, he was funny and charming. There was an amazing attraction. He made me feel like I was the most beautiful, wonderful girl in the world." Chloe sighed. "Three months later, we were married. A year later, we had Caiden."

"Do you regret not finishing school?"

"No. I went for one semester after we married. It was difficult to commute, and I wanted to spend time with Keith instead of doing homework." She smiled. "I love being a wife and mother. After Caiden started to school, I went to work at the preschool, mainly so Cassie could be around other kids. Her personality is different than Caiden. She's shy and needs the social interaction. Winn Timberman's little girl is just the opposite, bubbly and outgoing. They are best friends."

"Winn seems to be outgoing, too."

"He has a great personality." Chloe finished her cup of coffee. "So do you have a special guy in your life?"

She shook her head.

"I could fix you up with Winn. I think you two would hit it off great."

Andrea felt the blood rush into her face. She stood and rinsed out her cup. "I'm really not interested in a relationship right now."

Chloe brought her cup to the sink. "Okay, but let me know if you change your mind."

Andrea's cell phone buzzed. After a short conversation, she said, "I've got to go check on a horse that got tangled up in fence. Call if you need me."

***

Sunday morning Andrea put on her favorite jeans with the rhinestone pockets, a red plaid shirt over a red tank top, and her red boots. Taking extra time with her makeup, she wondered if Winn would be at church with his mother and her boyfriend. Would his little girl be there?

As she sat in church, she tried to listen to the message. The preacher talked about love: "You shall love the Lord your God with all your heart and with all your soul and with all your mind. This is the first and greatest commandment. And the second is like it: 'Love your neighbor as yourself.'" He went on to relate the parable of the Good Samaritan and practical ways Christians can demonstrate the love of Christ. He talked about a benefit roping being held at another church to help a cowboy suffering from leukemia. Andrea prayed asking God to help her be more loving to those around her, to put her love into action.

After church, she followed her parents to the back where the band stood greeting people. Before she could slip away, Chloe and her family walked up. Cassie was holding hands with a little golden-haired, green eyed girl with a cute turned up nose, sweet smile, and one dimple. Then Winn walked up, wearing a white Stetson, white starched George Strait shirt, Wranglers, a prize buckle, and black Justin boots.

Andrea's heart did a somersault into the pit of her stomach. He looked so good. She couldn't pull her eyes away from his. Then his mother walked up. She glared at Andrea with a ferocious mama bear expression. Her feathers ruffled like a mama hen ready to flog someone who got too close to her chick.

Winn picked up the little girl. "Andrea, this is my daughter, Charity. Chari, this is my friend, Andrea."

Charity smiled like an angelic cherub. Andrea's resolve dissipated. She wanted to hug the little girl, she wanted to hug Winn, to feel his arms around her. She reached out and touched the golden curls. "You are a beautiful little girl."

Charity giggled. "My daddy is han-some."

Andrea felt the blush, but it was the heat radiating from her pounding heart that alarmed her. She pulled away. "Um," turning around, she said, "Charity, this is my mother, Carmella, the candy lady."

Charity clapped her hands. "Did you bring cookies?"

Mrs. Travis appeared puzzled, so Andrea explained about the

cookies and the name "candy lady."

"If you come next week, I'll bring you some cookies," Carmella said to the little girl.

"Can I come next week, Daddy?"

Winn shifted his feet. Andrea felt the magical power of his gray eyes, like an electrical storm in her soul.

"I'll see you next week." Andrea waved as she walked away, avoiding eye contact with Chloe and Winn's mother. In the parking lot, she leaned against her pickup and took some deep breaths. *Calm down. Chill out. Get a grip.* Her hands shook as she opened the door and started the pickup. As she pulled onto the highway, she recited Proverbs 3:6 "In all thy ways acknowledge Him, and He shall direct thy paths." Which way do You want me to go, Lord? What do You want me to do? *Love your neighbor as yourself.*

She thought about the Good Samaritan parable. And who is my neighbor? *Winn Timberman.*

Please help me love him in a pure, Christian way. And Charity—I could love that little girl like my own. I know I could.

***

Around the dinner table with her family, Winn Timberman was the unspoken white elephant in the room. Finally her mother broke the silence. "That is the cutest thing that Winn's little girl calls me the candy lady."

Her husband winked at her. "You are the sweetest lady I ever did see, especially your candy kisses."

Andrea rolled her eyes. "Dad, really? You are not alone, you know?"

He leaned over and gave his wife a loud, smacking kiss. "I know. When can y'all leave?"

"I'm out of here." Andrea stacked her silverware on her plate and carried it to the kitchen. She wondered if aliens had snatched the dad she had known all her life. She liked the new, improved version, that's what she wanted someday, but right now she felt embarrassed and uncomfortable.

***

Winn felt awkward while Sam Howard held his mother's hand during dinner at the restaurant. He wanted her to be happy, but it was strange witnessing their public display of affection.

Sunday evening, Faith asked her son to sit with her on the back porch. "So, what do you think of Sam?"

"I've always thought he was an alright guy."

"What do you think of us being together?"

Winn walked to the porch rail and surveyed their property. Turning he said, "I just want you to be happy."

"I am happy. He wants to get married right away, but I think we should wait awhile."

"If you're sure you love the guy, why wait?"

"There's so many other factors to consider." She set the rocking chair in motion. "You and Charity."

"We'll be okay." Clyde came up and Winn rubbed the dog's

ears. "Just a few more days and you can get that cone off, old boy."

"Sam wants to live in his house, but his wife's presence is overwhelming."

"You want to live here at the ranch?"

She stopped the rocker. "No, your father's presence is here." She shook her head. "I kept this ranch for you. My name is on the deed, but I'll switch it to your name before I marry."

"Thanks, Mom." He leaned over and hugged her. "Charity and I will be fine."

"I can still watch her when you're on call, or when you have something else to do. I told Sam I hope to always be involved in her life."

"Of course you can, as far as I'm concerned."

She sighed. "One of these days you'll remarry, and everything will change."

"Some things won't change. And besides I don't have any plans right now."

"I saw the way Andrea looked at you, the way you looked at her." She tilted her head and put her hand on her cheek. "Anyone with half a brain could see the attraction, the magnetism. Time stood still."

"She doesn't even want to be friends right now."

"She may say that, but her eyes and body language say something entirely different." She laughed. "And you look like a love struck puppy."

"At least she's talking to me now."

"Yes, and she met Charity. Fingering her hair with tenderness, it's evident she loves kids, and her biological clock is ticking."

"Don't read too much into things, Mom."

"The handwriting is on the wall."

"Good night." He left her sitting in the rocking chair. As he lay in bed, he thought of everything his mother had said. It was true—the attraction he felt for Andrea was like a magnet pulling him toward her like the North Star, something steady, a guiding light, or was it something far away and unattainable? He knew she felt something for him, but it couldn't be as strong as what he felt for her. It couldn't be, or she wouldn't be able to stay away. She would want to be with him every minute of every day, the way he wanted to be with her.

***

After putting the kids to bed, Chloe snuggled next to her husband on the sofa and said, "Did you notice how Andrea and Winn reacted to each other?" When he didn't respond she continued, "The other day, after Winn took his dog home, she was asking questions about him. I thought she was interested, because he is pretty cute. Not as cute as you, of course. When I offered to fix her up with Winn, she said—"

Keith sat straight up and put his hands in front of him. "Whoa! Stop right there. Don't try to play matchmaker. Dr. Travis is your boss. Keep your relationship professional, or it might backfire."

She wrapped her hands around his large ones. "No, you stop! Do you know something I don't know?"

195

He shook his head. "I always try to mind my own business and stay out of other people's affairs."

"Affairs? Okay spill it. Tell me the truth, the whole truth, and nothing but the truth."

He pulled his hands away and wrapped her in a bear hug. "I love you, and that's the truth."

She wiggled to free herself from his hold. "Do not keep secrets from your wife. Tell me—the whole truth." He shook his head and tickled her.

Gasping she said, "Stop! Tell me, please?"

"Only if you promise not to say anything to Dr. Travis or Winn." She nodded. "And only if you promise not to ask any more questions."

"That's a hard one." She kissed him. "I'll try. Now tell me."

"They met in the tornado. He spent some time helping rebuild her clinic. They went out a couple times. She got mad when she found out he hadn't told her about Charity."

"That's it? She got mad because he didn't tell her about Charity?"

"Yes, I thought it was pretty dumb, too."

She shook her head. "Boy. She's got it bad. That wouldn't be a big deal unless she really cared."

"You promised to stay out of it." He cupped her face in his hands. "She has a really bad temper, so I mean it. Don't say anything. Don't ask any questions."

"Andrea has a temper? I don't believe it."

"Believe it. I saw it, and I don't want you to become a target."

"I'm not afraid. Besides, I don't need that job as much as she needs me." He raised his eyebrows, so she said, "I promise I won't say anything."

Chapter Twenty

Monday morning, Andrea just finished her Bible reading when Chloe came into the clinic. "Hey, I have some oranges and syringes so you can practice giving injections. I downloaded a video on the office computer to help you."

Chloe forced a brief smile. "Do you have anything else that you want me to do today?"

"Answer the phone, schedule appointments. Admit any emergencies that come in. I'll be at the Kane Ranch performing artificial insemination on some heifers, but you can call if you need me."

"Okay." Chloe clicked the video on the computer.

Andrea started for the door but stopped and turned around. "Are you alright?"

Without looking up, Chloe answered. "Sure, I'm fine."

Walking to the desk, Andrea said, "You don't seem like yourself. Is something wrong?"

Chloe focused on the computer screen and shook her head.

"Have I said or done anything to upset you?"

"PMS." She frowned but avoided Andrea's eyes.

"I have some amazing little herbal pills that have been around since the 1800's. They work wonders. Let me get the bottle." She disappeared into her private quarters and returned, handing a little brown bottle to Chloe. "These really help me. Go ahead. Take one. I buy them online, so I have plenty."

"Lydia Pinkham. What do they do?"

"They ease the discomfort, pain, bloating, and calm me down."

Looking at the label, Chloe asked, "Do you only take them when you have PMS?"

"No, they contain vitamins and natural nutrients. I take one every day and three of four when I *really* need them." She smiled. "They won't hurt you. I promise they'll make you feel better."

Chloe dabbed at the tears in her eyes. "Thanks."

"I won't pry into your private life, but if you need to talk, I have time to listen."

Chloe nodded. "I won't pry into your private life, either."

Andrea searched her face, but Chloe kept her eyes averted. Clearing her throat she asked, "Does this have anything to do with yesterday? With Winn?"

Tears clouded her eyes. "I promised Keith I wouldn't talk about it."

Andrea pulled a chair in front of the desk. "I met your husband the night of the tornado, and I saw him and Cassie at the Fourth of July street dance."

"Last night he told me about the tornado but not the street

dance."

"That's when I got mad and flipped Winn on his backside."
She pinched the bridge of her nose. "I have a black belt in Karate."

Chloe's eyes widened. "I hope you don't ever use it on me."

"I would never do that. Besides, I'm working on my temper."
She took some deep, relaxing breaths. "I felt like he lied to me."

"Winn lied to you?"

"Well, he didn't exactly lie, but he didn't tell me the truth,
either."

Chloe bit her bottom lip. "I promised Keith I wouldn't ask any
questions, wouldn't pry into your private life, but if you need to talk, I
have time to listen."

Andrea stood and put the chair back against the wall. "Have a
good day, and call if you need me."

***

As she drove to the Kane Ranch, Andrea felt like a deflated
balloon. She liked Chloe, thought they could be friends. *She and her
husband must think I'm a monster.* She shook her head. *Winn may
think so, too, but he still seems interested, very interested. That's why
I can't get involved. I'm too hot-headed, too impulsive, too critical
and judgmental.*

She thought about the lyrics of the kiddie song she used to
sing in children's church, "He's Still Working on Me". *Thank You,
Lord, for not giving up on me.* Then the words of one of her mother's
favorite hymns began playing in her mind:

"Have Thine own way, Lord! Have Thine own way!

Thou art the Potter, I am the clay.

Mold me and make me after Thy will;

While I am waiting, yielded and still.

Have Thine own way, Lord! Have Thine own way!

Wounded and weary, help me, I pray!

Power, all power, surely is Thine!

Touch me and heal me, Savior divine."

Yes, Lord, I've been wounded. I am weary. Please forgive me and heal me. Mold me and make me into the person You created me to be.

***

The rest of the week sailed by smoothly. Chloe and Andrea's relationship slipped back into a relaxed, friendly rhythm with no mention of Winn. On Saturday, Andrea asked her mother if they could bake cookies together. They invited Katie to join them, and they made snickerdoodles, chocolate chip, peanut butter, and oatmeal raisin, dividing them into Christmas tins.

"Katie, do you remember when we were in kids' missions' class and had Christmas in July? Collecting school and personal hygiene items for poor kids in inner cities?" Andrea asked.

"Yes, I loved decorating the Christmas tree in the children's Sunday School department in the middle of summer. My mom always made mittens, hats, and afghans, too."

"Yes, I never realized how truly blessed we were until our teacher read us those stories. When I was in college, I volunteered at a rescue mission. It was pretty depressing. When I was in vet school, I volunteered what little free time I had at an animal shelter. That was sad, too. People should be responsible and get their pets spayed or neutered."

Carmella sighed. "Some people love their animals but can't afford to get their pets fixed, especially if they're barely able to feed their kids."

"Then they shouldn't have animals," Andrea declared.

"In Chicago, there was always some kind of fundraiser to help sponsor pet adoptions, rescue organizations, low-cost immunization and spay and neuter clinics. The symphony held one mini concert a year to donate money for animal causes."

"Why couldn't we do that?" Carmella asked. "We could have a Travis Family concert. Perhaps your father and grandfathers would put on a benefit roping."

"That sounds great. I'll check into the legal requirements," Andrea said.

"Do you want me to take the cookies to church for Winn and his little girl, or do you want to do it?" Carmella asked.

"You do it since you're the candy lady. I'll take one for Chloe and her family. Katie can take some, and you can keep the rest." Andrea felt like her life was coming back together, her relationship with Katie mended, hope for a relationship with Winn, well, at least friendship.

***

The next day, Andrea and Carmella carried the cookie tins to the back of the church where the band gathered to greet people. Charity and Cassie walked up swinging their hands. Carmella leaned down to hand Charity the tin. "Here are the cookies I promised you."

The little girl threw her arms around Carmella's neck and said, "Thank you, Candy Lady."

Andrea stepped forward and handed a tin to Cassie. "These are for you and your brother. It might be nice to share with your mom and dad, also."

A wide grin spread across the little girl's face. "Thank you," she whispered in her timid voice.

Austin strode to his father. "Dad, can Caiden come home with us so I can teach him to rope?"

"We're going to Abuelo and Grandpa Dustin's house for dinner today," Brooks said.

Batting his long lashes Austin asked, "Abuelo, can my friend come eat dinner with us today so me and Grandpa Dustin can teach him to rope? Please?"

"Of course, if it's okay with his parents. Our house is always open to family and friends."

"I can bring him home if it's too inconvenient for you to drive back," Andrea offered.

Chloe gave her husband a questioning look. "No, we can come

back and get him. What time?"

"Maybe three?" Brooks said. "That will give the boys plenty of time to practice roping after they eat."

"We're eating in town with the Timbermans and Mr. Howard, so that should work," Keith said exchanging phone numbers with Brooks. "Thanks for the cookies, Dr. Travis."

"You may call me Andrea."

Winn picked up his daughter who said, "Hug, Andrea."

As Andrea returned the little girl's hug, Winn's breath brushed her neck. The closeness ushered in a sensation of intimacy, an overwhelming feeling of comfort and contentment. Andrea closed her eyes soaking in the solace. Charity giggled and pulled away. "I like you."

"I like you, too." Andrea's eyes met Winn's. Something lovely passed between them, something sweet and innocent. She remembered a scene from her favorite movie, *The Man From Snowy River* when Jim and Jessica first kissed. She wanted to kiss Winn, right there in church. She licked her lips and stepped back. "Well, I guess I'll see you next week."

As she left the church, she felt all eyes on her, burning a hole in her back. She hoped her family wouldn't say anything over dinner. Maybe having Caiden as a house guest would curb the conversation.

***

That afternoon over dinner, Winn felt the questioning glances. Thank goodness Charity and Cassie kept the conversation lively.

Nobody mentioned Andrea and what happened at church, well if anything did happen at church. Maybe he was the only one who felt the floor shake beneath his feet. His mother spent the rest of the day with Sam.

Charity fell asleep on the drive home. After putting her to bed, Winn flipped through the cable channels. Nothing captured his interest. Confined to the house, his pent up energy pressed him to pace the floor. Images of Andrea paraded through his mind. She said she wasn't interested, but the mixed signals perplexed him. Her wide eyes invited him into her soul. She licked her lips and her mouth parted, a clear prelude to a kiss. But then she left. Walked right out of church, the door slamming shut behind her. Should he call her? No, she was probably with her family.

His mother came in red eyed and sniffling. Rushing to her bedroom, she slammed the door behind her. When she didn't emerge after a few minutes, he knocked on her door. "Mom, may I come in?"

"No." She sniffled and blew her nose.

"Will you come out and sit on the porch with me?"

She opened the door, and he put his arm around her leading to the back porch. Sitting next to her on the swing he asked, "Do I need to go teach Sam some manners?"

"No."

"You want to tell me what's wrong?"

"We were at his house, talking about getting married." She sniffed. "I told him how I wanted to redecorate and change the house, so it would be ours, not his and his first wife's." She blew her nose. "He got mad and accused me of being bossy."

"Bossy, huh?" He hugged her. "Mom, you know I love you, right?" She nodded. "So don't take this the wrong way, but you can be bossy sometimes."

"He should understand that I can't live in that house as it is. It's like a shrine." She sobbed. "I think he still loves her and I'm just a replacement."

Aww, the victim mentality. "How long were they married?"

"Thirty years."

"And how long have you known him, dating I mean?"

"We've known each other for over ten years. We've been seeing each other personally for about six months."

He raised his eyebrows. "I didn't realize it had been that long."

"I didn't want to say anything in case nothing came of it."

The same reason he didn't tell Andrea about Charity. "How would you feel if I got married and my wife came in and changed everything in this house, your house?"

"But I'm still alive."

"Yes, and his wife is not." He inhaled deeply. "There are things about Janae I will always love, and we were only together a couple of years. Charity is a carbon copy of her mother, and I love her with all my heart. I think it says something about Sam that he loved his wife so deeply."

"But I don't want to live in her shadow."

"Do you think the house is what makes you feel that way?"

"Maybe. I thought he loved me, but now I'm not sure."

"Andrea is nothing like Janae, but I think I love her. What I feel for her is totally different than what I felt for Janae. I think a man is capable of loving more than one woman in a lifetime. Just like you loved Dad, and now you love Sam."

"You're right. I am a different person now that I'm mature. What I feel for Sam is a comfortable, peaceful feeling. What I felt for your dad was wild and reckless." She stood and walked to the porch railing. "It's not like I would throw her stuff out. I would let his girls go through their mother's stuff and take whatever they want."

"Have you met his girls?"

"Not yet."

"Maybe that's where you need to start. Tell him you would like to meet his daughters, to give them the opportunity to go through their mother's things and take what they want. You might want to wait on the redecorating until after you get married. Then you and Sam could do it together."

"Except for the bed. I wouldn't want to sleep in her bed."

"TMI, Mom. I don't want to hear about anything that personal."

***

That night after Charity and his mother were in bed, Winn walked out to the barn. He debated about whether to call Andrea. It

207

wasn't quite ten o'clock. He'd just call her cell phone. If his number was still blocked, he'd let it go. On the fifth rang she answered.

"Hello, Winn."

"Hey. I didn't know if the call would go through, but, um, I wanted to call and thank you for the cookies."

"You're welcome." She took a deep, relaxing breath. "Katie, my mom, and I baked them together, like we used to do years ago. I enjoy baking."

"I remember your chocolate cake. It was the best I've ever eaten."

"Thank you."

The only sound he heard were the crickets in the background. He cleared his voice. "Um, Charity took an instant liking to you."

"She is sweet. And beautiful." She took another deep breath. "I guess she looks like her mother."

"Yes, she does."

Andrea sighed. "When I was young, I wanted to be a blond. My complexion and blue eyes would go well with blond hair. My parents would never have allowed me to bleach my hair, but I almost did it in college. I made an appointment and everything."

"I'm glad you didn't. You're beautiful just the way you are."

"Thank you." Another prolonged silence.

"Well, I just wanted to call and thank you for the cookies."

"You're welcome."

"I guess I'll see you next Sunday." He stopped dead in his

tracks waiting for her response.

"Don't forget to bring Clyde in for his checkup. I need to take his drain tubes out."

"When should I bring him?"

"Just call the clinic tomorrow and make an appointment."

He sighed. "Could it be after hours, so I don't have to take off work?" *And so we could be alone?*

"Sure. Just let me know before you come, so I will be expecting you."

"Thanks." He kicked the hay. "I could bring you something from Dairy Queen, if you want."

"We can talk about that later, when you call, I mean."

"Okay." He closed his eyes and pictured her beautiful face, her full lips. "Good night, Andrea."

"Good night, Winn."

After the phone clicked off, he reached down and patted Clyde behind the ears. "You are a life-saver, Clyde, in more ways than one."

***

After they hung up, Andrea washed her face and gazed into the mirror. *I could be a blond, if I wanted to, but it would be such a hassle. My hair grows so fast, and my roots would be jet black. I'll have to think about it.*

When she lay in bed, she thought how good it would feel to kiss Winn good night. And to kiss him good morning. Then she prayed asking God to give her wisdom and discernment, to guide and direct her.

Chapter Twenty-one

Monday Winn called Andrea's cell phone at 5:30 PM. "I have Clyde and am headed your way. Would you like something from Dairy Queen?"

"I worked pretty hard today. I think an Xtreme Chocolate Blizzard sounds good, with a small burger."

"Would you like an order of French fries or onion rings?"

"Are you getting some?"

"Onion rings."

She laughed. "I'll just eat some of yours."

"Yes, I would be glad to share."

After he hung up, he felt warm all over. He loved her easy laugh. He felt comfortable with her. Yes, he would gladly share his onion rings with her. And his life, every part of his life, including his daughter.

***

Andrea took a quick shower. She donned a purple tank top that made her eyes look more purple than blue. She applied fresh makeup, finishing up with lip gloss as the buzzer rang. A smile spread across her face when she saw Winn making a face at the peephole. Opening the door, she asked, "Are you trying to scare me?"

"What? What you talking about?"

She giggled. "I saw those funny faces."

"Are you a peeper?"

"Only when someone rings my buzzer."

He contorted his face. "I was doing my pre-dinner exercises to get loosened up to eat."

She laughed uncontrollably. "Pre-dinner exercises? I've never heard of that."

"Try it. It helps relax your facial muscles."

She moved her lips, her jaws, inflated and deflated her cheeks.

"Beautiful." He smiled a tender, sweet smile. She thought he might kiss her, but he didn't.

"Let's eat now that we're loosened up. Then you can take care of Clyde."

"Walk this way."

***

He couldn't walk like her, with her smooth, easy rhythm, completely feminine, like a lady in waiting. She should be dressed in a long gown of satin and lace, but he liked her denim, or maybe the way the denim showed her shapely curves.

They talked and laughed through dinner as if nothing had happened, well, as if nothing bad had happened. He prolonged the meal as long as he possibly could.

"Okay, Clyde, are you ready to get your drain tubes out?" she asked.

Winn enjoyed watching Andrea work with the dog. Patient and gentle, the way she was with Charity and her nephew. When she finished, he asked, "When did you decide to be a vet?"

She straightened and rolled her shoulders before scrubbing her hands. "I always loved animals. Science and math were my favorite subjects. Celina was a great barrel racer, and she was artistic. Brooks was a great singer and guitar player. The only thing I was great at was academics." She dried her hands and rubbed lotion on them. "We took aptitude inventory tests in eighth grade. My results said I should be an animal trainer or veterinarian." She shrugged. "The men in my family are the best horse trainers in the world. I could never compete with them, so I decided to be a vet."

"You never wanted to be anything else?"

"The regular things every little girl wants to be: a princess, a real live Barbie, a movie star," she averted her gaze and added softly, "a wife and mother."

A lump formed in his throat. He would like to help her with the last two. "Most little boys want to be cowboys or policemen or firemen." He shuffled his feet. "I wanted to be a bull rider because that's what my dad was."

"But you have a little girl who already lost her mother."

He nodded. "Sometimes our priorities change."

"That's noble, as long as you don't resent giving up your dreams."

"I love Charity and want her to have a stable home. I want to be there for her, be a part of her life." He put his hands in his pockets. "Besides I could never be as good a bull rider as my dad." He winked. "I'm one heck of a lineman, lighting up people's lives."

"Yes, and saving people from tornados." She flashed him a smile that lit up his life.

***

On Tuesday, Chloe came bouncing into the clinic. "We're having Cassie's birthday party Saturday. Caiden begged to invite Austin so he wouldn't have to be the only boy at an all-girl party." She put her purse behind the desk and continued, "I thought you might like to come so your sister-in-law will know someone."

Andrea said, "Katie's never been shy."

"I'd really like you to come, too."

"It's a kid's party."

Chole rolled her eyes. "When preschoolers have parties, it's more about the adults than the kids."

Andrea licked her lips. "Who else will be there?"

Chloe focused on the ceiling like she was trying to get a picture of the guest list in her mind. "Keith and I, our parents, some other kids from the preschool and their parents, your sister-in-law, and you if you come."

"Some other kids from the preschool and their parents?"

Chloe nodded.

"Does that include Winn?"

"Well, Charity is Cassie's best friend." She sat in the desk chair. "Winn will probably help Keith grill the hot dogs and hamburgers, so you won't even know he's there."

Yeah, right. If he's there, I'll know it, just like he'll know I'm there. "I'll talk to Katie and let you know."

***

Saturday Andrea rode with Katie to Cassie's party. When they arrived, Caiden grabbed onto Austin and his rope, and the two boys disappeared behind the house. Andrea caught a glimpse of Winn in her peripheral vision and caught him sneaking stealthy glances at her. The women gathered around the picnic table while the men congregated in lawn chairs near the coolers and grill.

Charity hugged Andrea and held her hand in between games. The little hand in hers felt soothing, satisfying. She looked at Winn and their eyes locked. She felt the warmth spread from her heart to her smile. Instead of returning her smile, he looked away. *Was he upset? Should she turn loose of Charity's hand?* But when she tried, the little girl squeezed tighter. Andrea smiled down at the cherub. She would ignore Winn. She wouldn't disappoint the child.

After the games, the mothers fixed their children's plate. Charity looked up and said, "Will you fix my plate, Andrea?"

"Sure, sweetie." After giving Charity her food, she asked Katie, "Would you like me to hold Dallas while you fix your plate?"

Katie handed her the baby and walked to the food table. Andrea loved holding Dallas. Yes, she always wanted to be a mother, but she would need to be a wife first. At least that's the way it should

215

be. She could feel someone's eyes boring a hole through her. She looked up to find Winn staring at her. He didn't smile, and neither did she. She couldn't read his expression, but it didn't look angry. She held the baby until Katie finished eating.

When Andrea walked to the table next to the grill, Winn stood behind her. "Can I help you with your plate?"

"Thank you, but I can manage." He was standing so close she could feel his breath on her hair.

He lowered his voice and said, "Charity is quite charmed by you."

"I find her charming, also."

"I don't want her to get attached and be disappointed."

She felt the urge to cry. She fixed her plate and sat it in a chair next to Katie. "Chloe, may I use your restroom?"

"Sure. My mom's inside and she'll show you where it is."

Andrea closed the restroom door and leaned against it. *I don't want to get attached and be disappointed, either. God help me.* She wiped away the tears and splashed water on her face. She touched up her makeup, took some deep breaths, and returned to her chair. Her appetite gone, she picked at her food.

"Andrea, as soon as the kids finish their ice cream and cake, we'll leave," Katie whispered.

Andrea nodded. She watched Charity, the happy, bubbly, little social butterfly. Children are so trusting, so innocent. She wouldn't want to hurt the little girl, or any child.

When they said their goodbyes, Charity ran up to Andrea and hugged her legs. Lifting her sweet face she said, "I love you, Andrea."

Reacting without thinking, Andrea picked up the little girl and swung her around. Kissing the top of her head, she said, "I'll see you tomorrow."

"Will you bring cookies?"

Andrea laughed. "Not tomorrow." She carried the child to her father. Setting her in his lap, she said, "I'll see you tomorrow, Winn." He blinked, looking baffled.

Charity said, "One more hug."

Andrea hugged the child, her face close to Winn's, and said, "Thanks, I needed that." She smiled and walked away. *Yes, that's exactly what she needed.*

***

On the drive back to the clinic, Katie asked, "What happened between you and Winn today?"

Andrea turned to check on Austin, who was occupied with a video game in the back seat.

"Basically the same thing—he doesn't want Charity to get attached to me and then be hurt."

Katie nodded. "That's exactly how I felt with Brooks. I didn't want Austin to get attached just to be let down if Brooks decided to rejoin the band and hit the road again."

"Yes, but Brooks was his dad. He had a right to see him, even if he did end up leaving again."

217

"Austin would have been heartbroken if his dad had left, or if I had gone back to Chicago."

"I'm thankful things worked out for you and Brooks." Andrea drummed her fingers on the dash. "Charity is a friendly outgoing child. She likes attention. It's not necessarily about me."

"Don't be too sure. Before you get involved with his daughter, you need to figure out how you feel about Winn." Katie took her eyes off the road and stared at her sister-in-law. "If you're not interested in pursuing a relationship with him, then you need to back away from the little girl."

Andrea met her gaze. "I really like him. I'm just not sure what I want." *Liar, liar, pants on fire. You know you want to be with Winn.*

Katie gave her an all-knowing look. "Brooks and I will pray for you. In the meantime, go slow."

***

That night after reading her Bible and praying, Andrea lay awake thinking about Charity and Winn. Her own dad was gone more than he was home, but her mother, the backbone of their family, always read stories before bedtime prayers.

Andrea thought of some of her favorite stories, Dr. Seuss, *The Pokey Little Puppy, Frog and Toad, The Gingerbread Man, Paddington.* She would love to read to her children, someday. She would love to read to Charity. She wondered if Winn read to her or if he left that up to his mother. *God, I'm falling in love with Winn and his little girl.*

218

She prayed the Prayer of Jabez: "Oh that you would bless me and enlarge my territory!" *God I want a family. I think I want Winn and Charity.* "Let your hand be with me, and keep me from harm so I will be free from pain." *More than that, Lord, I don't want to cause pain or problems for Winn or his little girl.*

She recited her memory verse "In all thy ways acknowledge Him, and He shall direct thy paths." *Dear Lord, You are the potter. Mold me into who You created me to be. I hope that is a wife and a mother. If not now with Winn and Charity, then someday with someone you choose.*

Chapter Twenty-two

When she was ready for church, Andrea called Winn's cell phone. On the fifth ring he answered. "Hey."

"Hey." She took a deep breath. "I was thinking, since you have to eat, and I have to eat, maybe we could eat together—today, at Dairy Queen, with Charity."

She heard the distinctive click of a metal gate before he answered, "I don't know."

"We could go to Pat's or somewhere else if that would be better for Charity."

"I'm not sure what would be better for Charity."

"You asked if we could be friends." She inhaled deeply and whispered a silent prayer. "I'm ready to give friendship a chance."

"Yesterday Charity said she loves you, and she wants you to be her mother."

She couldn't stop the tears. That's what she wanted, too, wasn't it? "What did you tell her?" Her voice cracked.

"I told her kids don't get to pick their parents."

Andrea nodded. "Did that satisfy her?"

"No. One of the kids in her preschool class is adopted. He tells the other kids how special he is because his parents got to choose him." He sighed. "Charity thinks she should be able to pick her new mom since her real mom is dead."

"What did you say?"

"I told her I'm sorry, but it doesn't work that way."

"Could you tell her we can be friends? Maybe I could be her Aunt Andrea, like I'm Austin's aunt, because she doesn't have any aunts." She waited for a response. "Does she have any aunts or uncles?"

"No, Janae was an only child, too." She could hear him breathing deeply before he said, "This is why I didn't tell you about her right away. I don't want her hurt."

"I don't want her hurt, either." She blinked back tears. "I love Austin and Dallas. I love kids." She sniffled. "I already feel attached to Charity."

She could hear something banging. "The problem is . . . Charity and I go together."

She sat on her bed and lay back on the pillow. "I can't make any promises about how things might end, but I would like to try for a new beginning, starting slow, with friendship." She put her forearm over her eyes. "I realize you and Charity go together. I can't have one without the other, and I wouldn't want it any other way."

"So now you think we can be friends?" His gruff voice startled her.

"Yes, I hope so." She took a deep breath. "I like you. I like you a lot."

He exhaled deeply, like he had been holding his breath. "I like you, too, but I love Charity, first and foremost."

"That's one of the things I like about you." She sat up and rolled her shoulders to relax the tension. "So, will you ask Charity if she wants to eat at Dairy Queen with Aunt Andrea?"

"No." He exhaled deeply. "Let's leave the aunt part off. We'll just tell her that you are our friend—for now." She could almost hear the smile as the tone of his voice changed.

After she hung up, Andrea washed her face and reapplied her makeup. *Friends for now.*

***

Lord, I've prayed more the past few weeks than probably my whole life. I'm asking you to protect Charity. I'm willing to take a chance on getting my heart broke, but I can't stand the thought of that happening to my little girl.

On the drive to church, Winn told Charity they were going to eat lunch at Dairy Queen with Andrea. She clapped her hands and said, "See, I bet she wants to pick me for her little girl 'cause she doesn't have one."

"She is my friend, and she wants to be your friend. She likes you, but we can't talk about her being your mommy."

"Why not?"

"Because she is just our friend."

The light in her green eyes sparkled like emeralds. Her smile produced the dimple in her cheek. "If she was my mommy, she could

222

be your wife."

He laughed. "How old are you?" She held up four fingers. "You are too smart for your age." He winked at her in the rearview mirror. "We are only friends. We need to spend some time with Andrea, and become better friends, before we think about getting married."

"I'm thinking about it." The girl giggled.

"Okay, but we have to keep it a secret, like when you make a wish before blowing out your birthday candles. If you tell someone, it might not come true."

***

After church, Charity bolted from her dad and ran to Andrea, who picked her up and twirled her around. She cupped Andrea's face in her little hands, and kissed her cheek. "I love you, Andrea."

"I love you, too, Charity." She responded without thinking. Standing around the band, all eyes focused on them, like they were in the spotlight, center stage, in a dark theater.

Looking at her dad, the little girl scrunched her face into a wink. Turning to her grandmother, she said, "We're going to eat at Dairy Queen." Her grandmother raised her eyebrows and her jaw tightened.

"Oh, can I go?" Austin asked.

"We don't invite ourselves to eat dinner with other people," Katie admonished.

"Sure he can go, if it's alright with you." Andrea looked at

Winn for a response.

He flashed his smile and said, "Sure, the more the merrier."

"Can I Mom?" Austin batted his long lashes.

Katie looked from Andrea to Winn and back to Andrea. "Okay, but eat your dinner before getting ice cream."

Andrea tousled Austin's black hair. "Let's go."

Winn held Charity in his right arm, put his left hand on Andrea's back, and as they walked out the church doors, Andrea felt the laser stares burning her back.

Winn said, "Let's go in my pickup since Charity's car seat is there." Pulling out of the parking lot, he started laughing.

"What?" Andrea asked.

"That stirred up some dust."

She smiled. "Happy dust, I hope."

His eyes met hers, and she felt the electricity. "I hope so."

***

After putting Charity to bed, Winn's mother asked him about his lunch date. "It wasn't a date, Mom. We hardly even talked because the kids kept us laughing." He ran his fingers through his hair. "How was your lunch date with Sam?"

"Relaxing." She sighed. "He's trying to schedule a time when both of his girls can come here to meet me and go through their mother's personal things. If all goes well, we'll set a date for the wedding, and then we'll begin redecorating after we're married and settled in."

"Sounds like a plan."

"What are your plans—with Andrea, I mean?"

"No plans. We're just friends."

She raised her eyebrows. "Charity is too young to understand that friendships don't always last."

He shook his head. "I have some things to do outside." Once inside the solitude of the barn, Winn called Andrea.

"Hello, Winn."

"Hey. I just wanted to thank you for today."

"It was my pleasure. I really enjoyed spending time with the kids. They're so funny."

"Yeah." He closed his eyes and said a silent prayer. "I always enjoy being with you."

"Thank you," she said in a breathy voice.

Thank you? Is that all?

"Laughter is good for the soul." He could hear the hesitation before she said softly, "You lighten my heart and make me happy."

"Being with you makes me happy."

"Today was definitely a day of happy dust." She sighed. "What did your mom say when you got home?"

"I was home before her, and she didn't' say anything until Charity was asleep."

"Do you read to her?"

"What?"

"Do you read to Charity before bedtime?"

"Yes, I've been reading from my old children's Bible. Her favorites are baby Moses and baby Jesus. She loves babies."

"That's nice," she said in a singsong voice. "What did your mother say?"

"She asked about our plans." He took a deep breath. "I told her we are just friends—for now."

"That's what I told Katie when she called." She sighed. "She's such a romantic—her mind is already planning a wedding."

After an extended silence, in a tremulous voice he said, "Don't let her get together with Charity."

"Oh, my goodness, that would be double trouble!"

He sat on a bale of hay, wishing she were beside him. "Have you got a busy week planned?"

"Not too much so far."

"Maybe we can see each other sometime, this week, I mean."

"Maybe we can, since you have to eat, and I have to eat, maybe we could eat together." He loved her teasing tone.

"I never know where I'll be when, but I'll call you when I'm in the area." He pictured her full, moist lips and imagined kissing her. "Good night, Andrea."

"Good night, Winn."

***

After she hung up, Andrea lay on her bed, staring at the ceiling. *Thank You for today, Lord. It was a day of happy dust, better than fairy dust, because it was real. Today made my heart happy.*

After reading the Bible, she closed her eyes, but the racing of her heart kept sleep at bay. She thought about the list she made in high school when the youth group went through the "True Love Waits" class:

"Character. Honesty. Integrity. Loyalty. Work ethic. Thoughtfulness. Consideration. Humility. Patience. Kindness. Goodness. Faithfulness. Gentleness. Self-control."

Honesty is non-negotiable. She was angry when she thought Winn had lied to her. Actually, she realized at the time that he hadn't really lied, but he hadn't been completely honest, either. Now that she knew Charity and knew the story, she could understand his desire to protect her.

Winn possesses character, a good reputation and respect from people who know him.

Integrity—he seems sincere. He's definitely loyal to his daughter and mother, to his fellow linemen, and he works hard.

He's thoughtful and considerate of his mother, his daughter, and everyone else she's seen him interact with.

He's humble, maybe too much. He doesn't know how good looking he is—he definitely needs someone to boost his self-confidence.

He's patient, kind, and gentle with his daughter, with his dog, and with her.

Everything about him exemplifies goodness.

Self-control. *Yes, Lord, self-control is so important.* He hasn't even tried to kiss her, although maybe she's ready now.

She remembered when he told her Robin Hood was his hero, how the cowboys and linemen were a lot like knights, following the code of chivalry, fighting for what's right, heroes, risking their lives for others.

She turned on the bedside lamp and opened the nightstand drawer, pulling out the picture of the Christian knight wearing the full armor of God. "Dear Lord, I know Winn said he accepted you as Savior when he was younger, so he already has the helmet of salvation. Please help him put on the breastplate of righteousness, guard his heart, Lord. Help him to hold onto the shield of faith, to trust you completely. Help him to tighten the belt of truth, which holds everything else together. Help him to study and apply Your Word, which is the sword of the spirit. I'm glad he reads Bible stories to Charity. And feet shod with the gospel—use him to make a difference in this world.

"Yes, Lord, please help me to put on the full armor, also." She leaned on the pillow propped against her headboard and whispered the old hymn:

"Have Thine own way, Lord! Have Thine own way!

Thou art the Potter, I am the clay.

Mold me and make me after Thy will;

While I am waiting, yielded and still."

Yes, Lord, please make me into the person You created me to be. If it is Your will, make me into the person Winn would want and need to be his wife, the person Charity would want to be her mother. I don't want to hurt them, but I don't want to set myself up for a fall, either.

***

The next afternoon, Andrea drove to Lubbock to see the counselor. She told him about her interactions with Winn and Charity the past two weeks. "So I think I am ready to give the relationship a chance."

He nodded. "If the relationship progresses, I do couples counseling."

"Like pre-marital counseling?"

"Relationship counseling, dealing with personalities and temperaments, values and beliefs, goals and plans." He steepled his fingers. "In addition to that, I recommend pre-marital counseling for everyone."

She nodded and rubbed her hands down her thighs.

"This week in your notebook, I would like you to write down what you want in a relationship. Write down the qualities you admire about Winn. How closely he matches what you want. Think about the little girl. Being a full-time mother is much more difficult than just having a few hours of fun."

She nodded. "I probably won't make another appointment unless something happens with Winn. If things don't work out, I may need to talk with you. If things go well, we may come in for the relationship counseling."

He stood and shook her hands. "I do hope things work out well for both of you. I like him and think he's a fine young man."

Yeah, I hope things work out well, too, for all three of us.

That night she called Winn at 9:00. Her heart sped up at the sound of his voice. "Are you on call this weekend?"

"No, actually I'm not."

"I had to go to Lubbock today, and I saw an advertisement for the Science Spectrum Museum. I would like to take you and Charity and Austin this Saturday. I think it would be fun."

"Only if I can take you." She closed her eyes and pictured his smile. "I'll drive and I'll pay."

"But I'm inviting you."

"Thank you, but I'm old fashioned. The man pays—always."

She laughed. "Are you a chauvinist?"

"No, I'm chivalrous."

Her heart skipped a beat. "Like a knight in shining armor."

"More like a traditional cowboy with a Stetson, Wranglers, and boots."

She thought of how handsome he looked dressed up. "Okay, cowboy. Can you pick me up around 9:00 Saturday morning?"

"I can pick you up earlier if you would like to eat breakfast together."

"We'll need to eat lunch after the museum, so that's probably enough." She would like to eat breakfast with him, and lunch, and dinner, every day from now on.

"Andrea?"

"Yes?"

"Will you wear that purple dress you wore when we went to Lubbock and ate at Las Brisas Restaurant?" She could hear his irregular breathing. "I like the way it makes your eyes look."

Her heart flip-flopped. "Okay. Will you wear your white Stetson and white shirt?"

He laughed. "Yes, and I'll wear Wranglers and boots, too."

She was thankful he couldn't see the blush she felt. "Good night, Winn."

"Could I take you to dinner tomorrow or one day this week?"

"I can't eat Dairy Queen every day. What if I cook for you on Wednesday?"

"I'd like that."

After she hung up she prayed. *Lord, I'm asking You to give me wisdom and direction. I want a relationship with Winn. I want to be happy. If this is Your desire, let it happen.*

Chapter Twenty-three

Andrea called her mother Tuesday afternoon. "Are you by any chance making homemade tortillas tomorrow?"

"I hadn't planned on it, but if you want to come for dinner, I'll make you some."

"I was wondering if you can make some for me to bring home."

"Sure I can do that."

"If your garden is still producing squash, may I have a couple yellow and zucchini? And some fresh tomatoes?"

She laughed. "Why don't you just come for dinner?"

Andrea paused. "Um, I'm in the mood for green chili calabacitos, but I can't make tortillas like yours."

"I can cook for you."

Andrea paced in her break room. "No, I want to cook."

"Oh . . . that's a lot of food for one person," Carmella said in her silvery voice.

"I'll call you tomorrow and let you know when I can come, maybe around lunch."

"We'd love to have you join us for lunch if you have time."

"We'll see what tomorrow holds." *Yeah, I bet they're ready to give me the third degree.* Andrea hung up, finished writing her list, and headed to the grocery store.

When she returned home, she baked her famous chocolate cake with fudgy icing, famous within her family, anyway. She cooked the ground beef for the calabicitas, made Spanish rice, and put beans in the crock pot to cook.

***

"Yum," Chloe said sniffing the air as she walked into the break room Wednesday morning. "What are you cooking?"

"Beans." Andrea said, stirring the pot. "You may have a bowl for lunch if you want some."

Chloe nodded. "I might eat some with you."

"I'm planning to eat lunch with my parents, unless something comes up." Andrea told Chloe where she would be working this morning. "But call in case of an emergency."

A smile spread across Chloe's face, her muscles twitched as she suppressed a laugh.

"What?" Andrea asked with her hands on her hips.

"Nothing." A giggle escaped. "I'm minding my own business." The giggle turned into a laugh that shook her shoulders.

"Why are you laughing?"

"I'm sorry." The laughter seized her.

"Okay, spill it. What's so funny?"

"I promised Keith I wouldn't ask any questions or butt into your business."

Andrea turned her back, washing the ladle and scrubbing her hands. She dried the spoon and wiped at the counter before facing Chloe. "This is about Winn, isn't it?"

"Yes." She wiped her eyes and tried to regain her composure. "I haven't said anything, because I really am trying to mind my own business, but you should have seen the looks on everybody's faces when you walked out of church with Winn."

Andrea slapped the dish towel on the cabinet. "What does that have to do with this?"

"Are you cooking for Winn?"

Andrea nodded. "And that's funny because?"

"I don't think it's funny. I think it's exciting." Chloe leaned against the table. "Trying to keep it a secret is like trying to stop the West Texas wind."

"What was said after we left Sunday?"

"All I could hear was my two kids whining because they couldn't go with Charity and Austin."

"What are you and Keith saying?"

"He minds his own business and doesn't say anything, which is what he expects me to do." Chloe put her hands up in surrender. "You're my friend. Winn is Keith's friend. Charity is Cassie's friend. So it is kind of my business, and I just want y'all to be happy."

"Thanks, but we're just friends."

"Whatever you say," Chloe raised her eyebrows, "but I've seen the way you look at each other." She leaned forward with her palms on the table. "Everybody's seen it. There's no denying the attraction." She straightened. "And just so you know, Charity told Cassie she wants you to be her mother."

Andrea's brow furrowed. "Please don't tell anyone she said that."

She shook her head. "The child has no inhibitions. Everyone will hear about it if they haven't already."

Andrea frowned. "That's great."

"I hope it will be great." Chloe walked to the reception desk and turned on the computer.

Andrea gathered her things and left.

A little before noon, she pulled into the T-C Quarter Horse Ranch. Her mother stood at the stove cooking tortillas. A pot of red chili simmered on the back burner. Fresh summer and zucchini squash and tomatoes filled two bowls on the counter. "Can you step out on the porch and ring the dinner bell."

Her mother liked ringing the bell, even though the men knew when to come in to eat. Once they were seated at the table and her mother offered thanks, Gramps asked, "How has your week been?"

"Not as busy as I'd like but okay," Andrea answered.

Her dad filled his plate then asked, "How was lunch at the Dairy Queen Sunday?"

"Sweet." They didn't laugh at her joke. "You know, the ice cream was sweet, and the kids were sweet."

Abuelo said, "Ah, kids make life sweeter. I hope when Celina and her husband come back from Germany that this ranch is full of little vaqueros."

Andrea looked at her mother. "Is Celina expecting?"

"Not that I've heard." Her mother shrugged her shoulders. "Celina is very private and proper, so I don't ask her any questions."

Her father grunted. "I don't mind asking questions." He took a big gulp of iced tea. "What's with you and Winn?"

"What about respecting my privacy?" Andrea asked.

"Once a man and woman are married, what they do is no longer their parents' business." Her father stared at her. "You're not married, yet."

"Exactly. So don't go getting any ideas." She buttered a tortilla. "Subject closed."

Abuelo raised his bushy eyebrows as his handlebar mustache inched into an upward curve.

After they finished dishes, Carmella handed Andrea two plastic bags. "Take as much squash and tomatoes as you want."

"Thanks. Do you have some frozen green chili? I bought some canned, but that's not as good as the Hatch green chili you roast."

Her mother placed a bag of frozen chili in the bag with the squash. "Do you need anything else?" Andrea shook her head. Carmella hugged her and said, "If you need anything, call—anytime."

"Thanks, Mom. I will."

***

While Chloe manned the desk, Andrea took a shower, applied

her makeup and slipped on a purple tank top and her favorite glitzy jeans. At 4:30, she told Chloe she could leave for the day.

"I hope your dinner is as good as you look," Chloe said as she removed the keys from her purse.

"Me, too," Andrea said in a shaky voice.

"Is Charity coming, too?" Andrea shook her head. Chloe hugged her. "Relax and have fun."

"I'll see you in the morning."

"I'll be all ears." Chloe laughed as she walked out the door.

As she made the avocado tomato salad and finished cooking the clabacitas, Andrea prayed aloud, "Lord I hope I know what I'm doing. I'm trusting you to direct my path and give me discernment. I'm asking you to give me the desires of my heart."

When she heard the buzzer ring, Andrea removed her apron before looking out the peephole. Winn held a vase of purple daisies. Taking a deep breath, she opened the door. His smile lit up her heart.

"You look beautiful," he said, handing her the flowers.

"Thank you. The flowers are lovely." Closing the door she said, "You look especially handsome in your white shirt and Stetson." *Yes, and your Wranglers.*

He removed his hat and ran his fingers through his hair. "Something smells good and spicy."

She led him to the break room and placed the vase on the table. "I hope you don't mind that I don't have fancy dishes. I picked these up at the Dollar Store after the tornado."

"I don't care about fancy dishes, because I'm just a country boy."

After placing the food on the table, she sat across from him. "Would you mind holding my hand while I say grace. That's what my family does."

He reached across the table and covered her hand with his, strong and manly, calloused from hard work.

While they ate, compliments gushed between bites. The calabacitas had just enough peppery seasoning to give it a kick. The beans were thick, yet juicy. The tortillas were tender and flakey. The tomato and avocado salad was cool and refreshing. The Spanish rice was fiery. The gooey chocolatey cake was melt-in-your-mouth delicious.

"You act like this is the best meal you've ever had. Are you trying to sweet talk me?"

"No. Honestly, everything is perfect, including the company."

She stood and refilled their glasses, avoiding his eyes.

After they ate, they talked about their day over a cup of coffee. Winn said, "The co-op is keeping close tabs on Hurricane Harvey. It may be the worst hurricane to ever hit Texas."

"Well, at least those people have enough warning to evacuate, unlike a tornado."

"A lot of people are leaving. Others take hurricane warnings like we take tornado watches."

"Yes, but when we get an actual warning, we pay attention."

Andrea said, "I wouldn't want to live on the coast. Hurricanes have tornadic winds plus pouring rains and flooding."

"Yes, and power could be out for days or weeks."

"I'm glad you'll be safe and sound here."

"I'm on the list to go." He reached across the table and wrapped his hand over hers. "The brotherhood of linemen extends beyond our local co-op. One of our principles is cooperation among cooperatives. If a natural disaster strikes, a national team of lineworkers stands ready to help each other."

She swallowed hard. "When will you have to go?"

"It will depend on when it hits and how hard." His stormy eyes held hers. "I'll let you know when I get the call." He smiled. "Hopefully it won't be before Saturday. I'm looking forward to the museum."

When she said goodnight, she had an overwhelming urge to hug him, but she was afraid she wouldn't want to let go.

***

Hurricane Harvey hit Friday night. Saturday morning Andrea sat glued to the television. Images of torrential rain, flooding, first responder and citizen rescues tore at her heart. Weathermen predicted the slow moving system would continue to drench the coastline. The hurricane was only the beginning of the problems.

Later seated in Winn's pickup, she said, "I've been watching the news. The hurricane is really bad."

"Yes, but let's not think about it or talk about it. Today should

239

be a fun day for us and the kids."

Andrea tried not to think about the hurricane. She tried to focus on Charity and Austin, their wide-eyed excitement, their innocence, their sweet laughter. But every time she looked at Winn, the swirling emotions within her threatened to shatter her resolve.

Winn's cell phone rang while they were eating lunch at Buns Over Texas. He returned to the table with a grim expression on his face. Andrea started to ask, but he glanced at the kids and shook his head. He dropped her off at the clinic and whispered, "I'll call after I put Charity to bed."

She put her hand on his arm. "When do you have to leave?"

"In the morning, around six."

"Stay safe." She gave him a quick hug then stepped back.

He stood still, a confused expression on his face. He cleared his voice. "I'm always careful."

She opened the door and went inside without saying goodbye. She prayed, asking God to watch over him, to bring him back safely for Charity . . . and for her.

After pacing the floor, she drove to her family's ranch. She saddled her favorite horse and worked her in the arena. Then she rode through the pastures with Abuelo as they checked the stock tanks. He dismounted beside a small pond. "Let's rest the horses beneath the shade of this tree."

Andrea sat beside the pond, took off her boots and socks, rolled up her jeans, and waded in the cool water. "I guess you've seen the news, about the hurricane."

Abuelo nodded. "Yes, it is bad."

"Winn is going in the morning with some other linemen."

"That is a good thing."

"It's not a good thing. It could be dangerous." She fought the tears that seeped into her eyes.

Her grandfather draped his arm around her shoulders. "Life can be dangerous sometimes. We have to trust God to take care of those we love."

"I didn't say I love him. We're just friends." She sat down to put her socks and boots back on.

"We can love our friends. Your Gramps and me were friends in Vietnam." He broke a branch off the tree and began whittling. "We are still friends fifty years later."

On the ride back to the ranch, Abuelo said, "Before he goes, you need to tell Winn how you feel."

"I'm not sure how I feel."

"What does your heart say?"

"It doesn't say anything." She rode on in silence.

They unsaddled the horses and brushed them. Abuelo's horse nuzzled his neck. He laughed. "This horse doesn't speak in words, but he shows me his love. All I have to do is pay attention."

***

That evening, Andrea sent Winn a text. "I will be praying for your safety. I care for you. More than just a friend."

He replied. "I care for you, too. More than just a friend."

She sent him a happy face emoji. He sent her a happy face with heart eyes.

"After you put Charity to bed, would you like to come over and have coffee and cake with me?"

"I'll text when I'm on my way."

***

After reading to Charity, Winn told her he had to go out of town to help people whose electricity was knocked out during the hurricane. "They don't have any lights or TV. Their refrigerators and stoves don't work. I will try to call you every night, but my phone might not work, either. Gamma will be here to keep you company and read to you."

She threw her arms around his neck. "I don't want you to go."

Kissing her on her head, he said, "I will miss you, but I need you to be a big girl for Gamma. Can you do that?" She nodded. "Sometimes we have to think about other people, to help them when they need help. That's what linemen do. When the electricity goes out, we have to go fix it."

He told his mother he had some things to take care of. He texted Andrea to let her know he was on his way, and he prayed as he drove. He prayed for those affected by the hurricane. He prayed that God would keep him and his fellow linemen safe and bring him back home. He prayed there was hope for a relationship with Andrea.

Andrea opened the door as soon as he pushed the buzzer. Her

smile warmed his heart. "Come on in. Do you want anything else besides cake and coffee?"

Well, yeah, he'd like to take her in his arms and kiss her. "No, I'm not hungry, but I can't turn down your cake."

She fixed him a cup of coffee and chamomile tea for herself. Sitting across from him, she asked, "How many guys are going?"

"Six from our co-op, including Keith. There will be linemen coming from all across the country."

"What will you be doing?"

"Everything. Replacing poles and transformers, stretching line, whatever needs done."

She stared into her cup of tea. "It sounds dangerous with all that water."

"We are professionals trained to put safety first." He reached across the table and stroked her hand. "I have too much to live for to take any unnecessary chances."

She sighed. "Charity is the sweetest little girl. I enjoyed today."

"It was a good day. She couldn't stop talking about the museum, mainly you. 'Andrea did this' and 'Andrea said this.' She is quite taken with you."

"I feel the same way about her."

They talked and laughed about the day with the kids. Finally, Winn said, "Five o'clock comes pretty early. I still need to get my things packed, so I guess I should go."

She nodded and put their plates in the sink. When they reached the front door, she took his hand and stared into his eyes. "I will pray for you every day."

"Thanks." He felt himself drowning in the deep blue sea of her eyes.

She dropped his hand and hugged him, her cheek brushing his, her breath tickling his ear. Then she kissed him gently. On the lips. She stepped back. "Please be careful and stay safe."

He put his hands on her shoulders. Her eyes pulled him forward like a magnet. He kissed her softly, tenderly. She wrapped her arms around him, pulling him close, kissing him thoroughly. His head spun. Tremors tingled up and down his spine. The dam broke, and all the emotion he had kept bottled up overflowed into that kiss like a bolt of electricity.

He pulled his lips away and gazed into her eyes. "I love you, Andrea."

She closed her eyes, dropped her arms, and opened the door. "Goodnight, Winn."

Stepping through the door, he said, "Good night, Andrea."

His heart beat erratically. He could hardly insert the key in the ignition because his hands shook like the rattler on a snake. *Goodnight, Winn? That's all she could say after I declared my love for her?*

Chapter Twenty-four

Andrea's phone chimed at 5:30 AM. The text read, *"I hope you have a good day. Thoughts of you kept me awake all night, but they were happy thoughts."*

She smiled and responded. *"All that sugar before bed. Happens to me sometimes, too."*

"I just wanted to let you know I'm thinking about you."

Her heart flip-flopped. *"Can you talk?"*

"Not now. No privacy."

"K. I had trouble falling asleep, but then I had sweet dreams."

"Want to tell me about them?"

"Not now. Stay safe." She added an emoji kissy face with a heart.

He sent her an emoji wearing a cowboy hat with a big smile.

"Get some zzz's while you're riding in the truck. Bye"

"Later"

She reread the texts several times. *Dear Lord, please keep him safe.*

After she showered and dressed, Andrea read her Bible and ate a yogurt before heading to church.

***

During the announcements, the pastor said he had been contacted by a cowboy church outside of Houston that had opened their doors as an evacuation center for people with animals. "Horses are being sheltered in the covered arena and pens. In addition to bedding, personal hygiene items, clothing, bottled water, and non-perishable food, they need horse and dog food, as soon as we can gather it and get it down there. The Blackwells have volunteered to take a stock trailer down Wednesday, which will give us a few days to collect donations. If anyone wants to help, meet at the back of the church after service."

Andrea's father and grandfathers volunteered to donate hay. After lunch, Andrea drove her mother to Lubbock. Carmella filled two grocery baskets full of water, peanut butter, cereal bars, crackers, canned meats, individual serving bowls of fruit, and microwavable macaroni and cheese, plastic spoons, toothbrushes, toothpaste, hairbrushes, combs, shampoo, conditioner, body wash, hand soap, lotion, and various sizes of disposable diapers and underwear.

"Mom, you don't have to buy everything. Other people will bring things, too."

"God has blessed us, so we can bless others." She shook her head. "I can't imagine not having the basic necessities, especially clean underwear." Before she checked out, she added a couple of kids' themed beds-in-a-bag, one queen-size bedding set, and pillows.

***

Monday morning Chloe came into the clinic wearing a frown

246

and downcast eyes. Andrea said, "A frown is just a smile turned upside down."

"I miss Keith so much. I can't sleep without him beside me. The kids are cranky, and even the dog mopes around with his tail tucked between his legs."

"That bad, huh?"

Chloe rubbed her tired eyes. "You have no idea."

Andrea nodded. "Have you talked to Keith?"

"He sent me a quick text this morning." She rested her cheek in her hand. "Have you heard from Winn?"

"A text message yesterday before he left and a quick one this morning."

Chloe turned on the computer. "You know what they say, 'Absence makes the heart grow fonder.'"

Andrea shrugged.

The next two days, they watched the news every free minute, glued to the heartrending images of destruction and loss. With the guys working 15-hour days, the short texts were few and far between.

Andrea's anger flared when she saw rescue workers freeing dogs that had been chained to trees and porches, left behind by their owners. "If they had time to get out, they had time to take their animals with them."

Chloe shook her head. "Some people are heartless."

Andrea called the Humane Society in Lubbock. Although she didn't have much money, she wanted to help in some way. They told her they could house some dogs and cats, but they needed help with transports. She drove to her family's ranch and asked if she could take one of their horse trailers to bring rescued dogs back to the Lubbock Humane Society. "I can use the portable kennels I got while I was working here after the tornado."

"It wouldn't be safe for a girl to go down there alone. All kinds of thugs are looting and stealing whatever they can get their hands on." Her father shook his head. "Besides, you have a business to run."

"I'm not a girl. Gramps, Abuelo, could you go with me? We could leave tomorrow. The Humane Society will set up the rendezvous point at College Station, and we could come back Friday or Saturday."

"Where will you sleep?" Gramps asked.

"In the cab of the pickup? The dorms at A&M are full of evacuees."

"No way would I allow that." Gramps spit tobacco in a cup.

Andrea's face contorted. "If you won't let me take a trailer, I can just take my pickup. I can take care of myself."

"We will go with you and make sure you are safe," Abuelo said in his smooth voice. Looking at her father, he said, "It's a good thing she wants to do."

Gramps spit out a wad of tobacco. Wiping his mouth, he said, "Get your stuff together. We'll pick you up in the morning at five."

***

The next morning her grandfathers picked her up in their dually pulling a brand new living quarters horse trailer. "Where did you get this?" Andrea asked.

"As soon as you left yesterday, your dad drove to Lubbock and bought it. He's been thinking about replacing the one he lost in the tornado," Gramps said, opening the gate of the horse trailer. "Your kennels are loaded, and your dad also bought some animal carriers for cats or small dogs."

"But he gave me the money he got from the insurance company for his old trailer," Andrea's voice cracked with emotion.

Abuelo put his arm around her shoulder. "Nieta, you are our treasure. We would do anything for you." He hugged her. "We were poor when we started our ranch, but not now. We have all worked hard, been wise with our money, and God has blessed us. Besides, we need this trailer to take our horses to shows and sales."Abuelo dropped his arm. "Let's go save some animals."

***

Gramps drove four hundred miles south to College Station. Andrea texted Winn and told him where she would be. *"If you could get away, I can drive somewhere to meet you tonight or in the morning before we leave."*

Winn didn't answer her until 8:30 that evening: *"I would love to see you, but I don't want you to drive by yourself. The area is crawling with criminals."*

"What if Gramps or Abuelo come with me?"

"Let me see if I can get a truck, and I'll get back with you."

An hour later he texted and told her he would meet her half way. Gramps decided to go with her while Abuelo stayed with the trailer. Winn's supervisor drove the co-op truck. When they pulled into the truck stop, the two older men went inside for a cup of coffee.

Winn and Andrea sat in the pickup. He took her hand and whispered. "It's been hard to concentrate because all I can think about it is you."

She put her hand on his cheek and kissed him tenderly. He wrapped his arms around her and kissed her completely, sending tingles up and down her spine. He pulled his lips away and caressed her hair. "I love you, Andrea, and I'm willing to wait until you're ready for a relationship."

She giggled. "I think we already have a relationship." She pulled away and took hold of his hands. "I have something to tell you."

"I don't care about the past. I only care about the future."

"Please, just listen and don't interrupt." Taking a deep breath, she said, "Being back at College Station has brought back some painful memories."

"You don't have to talk about anything that hurts." He kissed the tears on her cheeks.

She shook her head. "I need to do this." She told him about Hunter and the anger she had harbored for two years. She told him about the counselor and working on anger management.

"Do you know where the guy is now?" His heavy breath sounded like an angry bull.

She caressed his face. "It doesn't matter. He doesn't matter." She sighed deeply. "You matter."

"I would like to break that guy in two."

She shook her head. "That's why I didn't tell my family. I didn't want anyone I love to get in trouble for hurting him, and they would have, at least my dad and Gramps." She wrapped her arms around his shoulders and pulled him close, her cheek resting against his. "Can you forgive me for getting so mad at you for not telling me about Charity when I wasn't honest and didn't tell you about that guy?"

"I understand. Charity is an important part of my life and always will be. That creep wasn't part of your life and never will be." He kissed her forehead.

"I have one more thing to confess."

"You don't have to say anything else."

"Yes I do." She cupped his face in her hands. "I love you, Winn Timberman." And she kissed him.

***

The next morning Andrea signed the final release forms for the rescue animals and headed back to the trailer. Hunter appeared behind a bush and stepped in front of her. "Well, you look as good as ever." He reached out and touched her hair. "We have some unfinished business."

"The only unfinished business would be filing assault charges against you." She tried to push his hand away, but he fisted her hair and jerked her head backwards.

"You want me and you know it. That's why you didn't file a report two years ago."

She kneed him and flipped him on the ground. Taking deep breaths, she tried to control her anger. "I'm going to walk away. If you know what's good for you, you'll stay down."

He laughed maniacally. His glazed eyes looked like a crazed person. How could she have ever thought he was good looking? As he started to stand, she braced herself for another attack. Hearing footfalls behind her, she turned to see Gramps and Abuelo coming.

Gramps pulled his glock and pointed it at Hunter. "Go ahead, punk, make my day."

Andrea almost laughed. "It's okay, Dirty Harry. He's not going to get up."

Abuelo put his arm around her. "Do you know this man?"

She looked from Abuelo to Gramps. "If I tell you something, do you promise not to do anything foolish?"

"Tell us," Gramps said, keeping the gun pointed at Hunter's heart.

Andrea shook her head. "Not unless you promise me."

"We promise not to do anything foolish," Abuelo said.

By this time, a group of Humane Society workers and A&M students surrounded them. A policeman walked up, gun drawn, and told Gramps to drop his weapon.

He laid his gun on the ground and said, "This man attacked my granddaughter."

"That's a lie," Hunter said as he stood behind the policeman.

"He grabbed me by the hair. Look, he just wiped strands of my hair on his pants." The policeman looked at Hunter, examining his clothes. Andrea continued, "We went to vet school together. We went out. Once. He used Ketamine to drug me. It's an animal sedative that can be used as a date rape drug."

The policeman asked, "Did you file charges?"

"No. Some fellow classmates intervened and took me to their apartment. They thought I was drunk and needed to sleep it off. By the time I was coherent, it was too late. The drug passes through the system quickly, so I couldn't prove it." She could see the tension building in Gramps as his jaw tightened and twitched. She took hold of his hand. "Gramps, that was two years ago. I'm alright now. I've gone to counseling and worked through it."

He stepped toward Hunter. Through clenched teeth, he said, "I think *he* needs worked over and worked *through*."

Andrea tugged on his hand. "Abuelo, please help me."

Abuelo stepped in between Gramps and Hunter. "We are leaving now. Thank this nice policeman for your life. If you ever come near my granddaughter again, you will pay for what you did, and I won't use a gun."

"Officer, did you hear that threat? Arrest these crazy people, all of them."

Several people stepped forward stating they witnessed the attack on Andrea. "Ma'am, do you want to press charges?"

Andrea shook her head. "No. You have more important things to do, and so do we."

Gramps produced his Concealed Carry License. "On the ranch we have to be prepared for coyotes, copperheads, or rattlers. In town, we need to be ready for two-legged snakes."

An hour later they were on the road. Andrea said, "Abuelo, I thought you were the calm, gentle one."

"The calm, gentle one?" Gramps gave Abuelo a sideways glance. "He didn't win all those medals in Vietnam for being gentle."

"I am always calm, but I would give my life to protect my family," Abuelo answered.

"That's why I didn't tell any of you. Can we just forget it? I don't think Mom and Dad need to know."

Gramps drummed his fingers on the steering wheel. "We won't tell them if you promise to tell us if you ever see or hear from that twisted twerp again?"

"Twisted twerp?" The tension broke, and she laughed. "I love you both and am so thankful you are my grandfathers."

Abuelo's moustache inched upward beneath his smile.

Chapter Twenty-five

The next week, Andrea and her family began planning a roping event to raise money for the Humane Society and local rescue organizations. The highpoints of her days were the morning and evening texts from Winn. Her heart warmed when he ended each text with "I love you." And it felt so right to tell him she loved him, too.

Winn's humor turned every dangerous situation into a funny story. *"I felt like the chainsaw massacre-er, whacking away the trees to get to the downed power lines."*

"Today I was on top of the world. Well, actually just 30 feet in the air overlooking the new Houston waterfront."

"I went deep-sea fishing, splashing through rain-slicked roads, rescuing water-logged fish."

"A new adventure today. Rode in an amphibious vehicle to retrieve renegade lines that decided to go scuba diving."

"Witnessed a transformation today. A little creek became a raging river. Want to go whitewater rafting with me?"

"Monster mosquitos moved in from Mexico. We got nets from a Safari store to save us from being eaten alive."

***

On September 5, the evening news reported a lineman had

been electrocuted. Andrea immediately texted Winn. After receiving no response, she called Chloe. "Are you watching the news?"

"Yes, I already called Sam Howard. The lineman was from another state. Our guys are okay."

"Thank God!" *Our guys. Yes, thank You, Lord.*

"Winn is your guy, whether you know it or not."

Andrea smiled to herself. "I know."

"Did Winn tell you the funny story about the woman with the sign on the side of the road?"

"No, he didn't tell me that one."

"Well, evidently when they drove into a residential area, they saw a scantily dressed woman standing alongside the road, holding a sign that read, 'Hot single female looking for electrifying lineman.'" She giggled. "All the guys pointed at Winn and said he was available." She laughed. "Keith said Winn turned every shade of red and purple." She cackled. "He stood up and yelled, 'I'm not interested. I'm taken.'" A snort interrupted her laughter. When she caught her breath she said, "Then the guys really harassed him, wanting to know who would have him. You know how guys are."

"Did he tell them about me?"

"I don't know. That's all Keith said."

"Well, I'll see you in the morning." Andrea wondered what Winn said about her.

That night she lay in bed, staring at the ceiling, worrying about Winn's true feelings for her. When her phone rang, she closed her eyes and whispered a silent prayer. "Hey, Winn."

"Hey. I just needed to hear your voice. How was your day?"

Her heart almost jumped out of her chest. "We've been busy planning the benefit roping. We kept some of the overflow dogs at the ranch, and I have a couple at my clinic. I may keep one little shaggy mutt if she's not claimed. None of them were chipped."

"You have a good heart. That's one of the many things I love about you."

Do you really love me? "Do you have any funny stories? They make my day."

"Na, not today."

"I saw the news report about the lineman who was electrocuted." Her voice wobbled.

He cleared his throat. "He's from out of state, but we mourn any loss in the brotherhood." He exhaled a deep breath. "All linemen are well-trained and highly skilled. Safety is a priority, but on rare occasions accidents happen. It's tragic, and we all feel for his family. But don't worry about me. I have too much to come home for. I won't make any slipups."

"I prayed for his family. I'm praying for you constantly." She took a deep breath. *Let's lay it on the line—get it out in the open.* "Let's talk about something funny. What about the girl with the sign yesterday? You didn't tell me about that."

"I didn't think that was funny."

She sat up and paced her bedroom. "Chloe thought it was

hilarious."

"Sounds like you've already heard it."

She flopped on her bed. "I'd like to hear your side."

He cleared his throat. "Some people cheer when they see us, because they know we're there to restore their power. Others yell and curse, because they don't think we've worked fast enough. That woman was ridiculous."

"What did she look like?"

"With her Daisy Duke shorts and halter top, she looked like a walking advertisement for something I'm not interested in." His voice sounded gruff.

"What did you tell the guys about me?"

"I told them I found the most beautiful girl in the world," he cleared his throat, "the girl I'd like to spend the rest of my life with."

The words were like honey to her heart. "I love you and can't wait for you to come home." Her voice cracked.

"I love you, too. Good night."

"Good night, Winn. Sweet dreams."

He'd like to spend the rest of his life with me? God, I think that's what I want, too. She knew she would have sweet dreams.

***

The next morning, Winn called and talked to his mother. "How are things going with you and Sam?"

"He has been wonderful helping me take care of the stock. He's patient with Charity."

"When are his daughters coming?"

She cleared her throat. "They are both busy, and it's hard for them to get away. We were thinking about them coming the first weekend in October. They can spend Friday and Saturday sorting through their mother's personal things." Her voice sounded brittle. "Then we thought we could get married Sunday afternoon. Before the girls go back home." She took a deep breath and paused. "What do you think?"

"I think that's great." He laughed as relief washed over him. "I mean you love him and he loves you. You're both mature adults. You know what you want, so why waste time?"

"Thank you." She blushed. "We don't need a big ceremony, just our kids and maybe a few friends. His brother Donald came up from Houston. He's staying with Sam because his house was damaged in the hurricane. He'll go home after the wedding."

"Andrea and I have been talking," his voice sounded low and thick with emotion. "She was here last weekend picking up rescued animals to take to the Lubbock Humane Society."

"Yes?"

"I love her, Mom. I'm going to ask her to marry me."

"How does she feel?" she asked, her voice tremulous.

"She loves me, too. I knew she did even before she said it." He took a deep breath. "I would like to get married right away, but I don't know when she'll be ready."

Faith fought back tears. She wasn't sure if they were happy, sad, or fearful tears. "Well, um, most girls want a big wedding, the first time around. That takes time to plan."

"Whatever she wants is okay by me."

"I love you, Winn. I pray for the best for you and Charity."

"Love you, too. Can you wake her up so I can talk to her?"

After a giggly conversation with his daughter, a breakfast burrito, and a large cup of coffee, Winn was ready to face another challenging day.

***

That evening, he called Andrea. "An exclusive country club opened their doors to honor the linemen. They already had an appreciation day for fireman and one for policemen. We could swim in the junior Olympic-size pool, sit in the sauna, unwind in the whirlpool, and take showers. The long hot shower was the best, much better than the showers we've been taking at truck stops." He laughed. "The dining room was even fancier than Las Brisas Restaurant. They served us vichyssoise—a French potato soup, Caesar salad, prime rib, asparagus with almonds, and Baked Alaska. The food was good but too fancy for my taste. I'll never belong to a country club, but I would like to have a pool and hot tub someday."

"Me, too. Those are the only things I liked about living in an apartment."

"I hated living in an apartment when I went to Tech. I like my privacy, the simple life, and home cooking. I'd rather have your chocolate cake than Baked Alaska any day."

"I'll have a chocolate cake ready when you get home." She closed her eyes and inhaled, wishing his scent could be transported through the phone. "When do you think you might come home?"

"I'm hoping Saturday or Sunday."

Her heart rate sped up. "When will you know for sure?"

"About 280,000 customers were without power, 2,100 utility poles, and 55 transmission structures were damaged or destroyed. We've made great progress. If we're at 95 percent restoration, we can leave. Other crews will come in and help the locals with the rest."

"Will you call me as soon as you know?"

"You'll be the first one I call."

"I love you and can't wait to see you."

"I love you, too, Andrea. Good night."

As she lay in bed, she imagined their reunion. She couldn't wait to kiss him again. She knew she wanted to spend the rest of her life with him. She hoped he would propose. If it wouldn't be too bold or audacious, she would propose to him.

Chapter Twenty-six

Friday evening Winn called Andrea. "We got the word. We're heading home in the morning," he said in a husky voice.

She squealed. "Oh! I'm so happy! I can't wait to see you!"

"I'll have to go home first, to unload, cleanup, take care of things around the place, and spend some time with Charity." He lowered his voice. "As soon as I get her to bed, I'll head to your place. We'll have the rest of the evening together."

"Okay. I'll be waiting for you."

He heard the disappointment in her voice. "We can go somewhere, for a late dinner or something, or we can stay at your place and talk."

"How about just coffee and cake here, at the clinic?"

"I'd like that." He looked up at the sky. "Can you look outside, at the sky I mean?"

She opened to the front door and walked outside. "The moon is big and bright."

"Can you find the North Star?"

"Yes, I see it."

"For a long time, I've been adrift in the sea of life, with no direction, no goal," He said in a breathy voice. "You are my North

Star, my guiding light in the darkness. I love you." He closed his eyes and said a silent prayer.

Tears pooled in her eyes. "That is the most beautiful thing anyone has ever said to me. I didn't know you were so poetic."

"You're the most beautiful thing that has ever happened to me. You put a song in my heart, the pep in my step, the lyrics in my language." He laughed. "Maybe that was a bit much."

"You are my knight in shining armor. My Robin Hood. My hero in a hard hat. My fantasy come true."

"Whoa, don't lift me up so high—that would be a long way to fall." He felt unworthy of her praise. Thinking like that could only disappoint her.

"I don't think you know how special you are." She sighed deeply. "But we're going to work on that. Beginning tomorrow night."

He didn't know how to react. "Okay, then. I better go try to get some sleep before tomorrow."

She giggled. "Yes. You need your sleep. We have lots to talk about. Good night." She made a kissing noise. "I love you."

"Good night. I love you, too."

After he hung up, Winn walked around the truck stop, too wired to go to sleep. *Wow, God. I've been praying about Andrea and me. We've only known each other a few months. I've tried to be patient and wait on You to work things out. Are we moving too fast now? Please give me wisdom and direction.*

***

Charity squealed with delight as she ran into her dad's open arms. They both laughed as he swung her around. "Did you miss me, Baby Doll?"

She spread her arms wide. "I missed you this much."

He kissed the top of her head. "I missed you, too."

She took his face in her hands. "Did you miss Gamma?" He nodded. "Did you miss Clyde and Fluffy?"

He smiled. "Not as much as I missed you and Gamma."

She closed her eye into a wink. "Did you miss Andrea?"

"Yes, I did." He kissed her forehead. "Did you miss her?"

"Yeah, I only saw her at church. Can we go to Dairy Queen tomorrow? With Andrea?"

"I'll ask her later." He put her down. "Right now, I need to take a shower."

She scrunched her little turned up nose. "Yeah, you're kinda stinking."

He laughed. "It was a long ride home. That truck was hot."

"Cassie missed her daddy, too." A smile lit up her angelic face, and her eyes danced. "Maybe we can all go to Dairy Queen tomorrow."

He ruffled her hair. "We'll see."

He hugged his mother. She pushed him away and said, "Charity's right. You are kinda stinking."

After dinner, he read to Charity, and they said their prayers.

"Good night and have sweet dreams."

"Can you read me some more stories? I've really missed you."

"I know Gamma has read to you every night. If you want to go to Dairy Queen tomorrow, you need to go to sleep now." He pulled the pink comforter up to her chin and turned out the light. In the soft glow of the nightlight, she looked like an angel. *Thank You, God, for the gift of this precious little girl.*

He walked into the living room and kissed his mother on the cheek. I'm going to see Andrea. I'll see you in the morning."

She nodded and wiped at the tears pooling in her eyes.

"Why are you crying?"

"I don't know." She shrugged. "I love you and want you to be happy."

"Thanks." As soon as he was in his pickup, he called Andrea. "Hey I'm on my way."

"I'm ready and waiting." He could hear the smile in her voice. *Lord, please don't let me mess this up.*

***

Andrea stood at the window. She opened the door before Winn had a chance to ring the buzzer. Taking his hand, she pulled him inside closing the door behind him. She cupped his face and kissed him gently.

He wrapped his arms around her and pulled her close. "I love you, Andrea." He returned her tender kiss. She put her hands on his head, running her fingers through his hair, and kissed him

265

passionately. It felt like the Fourth of July—fireworks exploding, the ground shaking. The song *Waltz Across Texas* played in her mind, and she swayed with the music.

He pulled away. "Wow, just wow," he gasped.

She tried to kiss him again, but he said, "I think we need to sit for awhile."

"Whatever you say." She took his hand and led him to the break room. "Would you like some yogurt?" She grinned.

"What about the cake?"

After she cut the cake and fixed the coffee, she sat across from him. Taking her hand in his, he said, "Let's pray. Dear Lord, thank You for bringing me home safely. Thank You for this food. Thank You for bringing Andrea into my life. Be with us and guide us. Amen."

"Amen," she said.

Winn stroked her hand with his thumb. "I missed you so much. I can't imagine my life without you."

She tried to blink back tears. "Me, too. I mean, me neither. I mean, I love you."

Holding her hand, he got on his knees in front of her. "Andrea, will you marry me?"

"Yes, yes, right away." She pulled his face to hers and kissed him.

Pulling back, he asked, "Right away? Don't you need time to plan a wedding?"

She stroked his hair, his cheek. "No. I don't need or want a big wedding. I just want you. And Charity." She got on her knees beside him and kissed him so hard, they both fell over. She giggled through the kiss. "I'm sorry. I didn't mean to get so carried away."

She stood. "Wait here. I'll be right back." She returned and handed him a piece of paper. "This is the list I made in high school. You're everything I want in a husband."

Sitting in the chair, he shook his head. "I'm afraid I don't measure up."

She sat in his lap and wrapped her arms around him. "I think you do. The question is—do I meet your expectations?"

"You are far more than I could ever imagine." She kissed him again. Pulling away he said, "We need to stop, because there is a limit to my self-control."

"So let's get married right away."

"Are you sure?"

"I know that I know that I know." She returned to her seat across the table. Taking a sip of her coffee, she said, "I told you about Hunter and my anger."

"We don't need to talk about that ever again."

She took his hand. "There's more I need to tell you." She took another sip of coffee. "I saw him last week in College Station." Winn's eyes narrowed. "It's okay." She told him what happened. "So many times over the past two years I've imagined seeing him. I've imagined kicking the stuffing out of him, breaking his neck, even shooting and killing him." She shuddered. "I know that doesn't sound very Christian. The fact that I could control my anger proves that God has healed me, and I'm ready to move on with my life. My life with you."

"Okay. Do you want to drive to Lubbock and get married tonight?" He raised his eyebrows.

"When I say right away, I mean after the benefit roping."

"My mom and Sam Howard are planning to get married the first weekend in October."

"Two weddings in one month would be too much. What about the first weekend in November? Or Veteran's Day? Then it will be easy for you to remember our anniversary."

"Oh, don't worry. I'll remember such an important day." His eyes twinkled and he kissed her on the cheek.

"When do you want to talk to my parents? We're old enough we don't need their permission, but I would like to have their blessing."

"When do you want to ask Charity? She wants us to go to Dairy Queen tomorrow."

She laughed. "Once we ask her, everyone will know, so we better ask my parents first. What about in the morning? They'll be up by five or six."

"Okay, I'll pick you up at five-thirty."

***

The next morning, Andrea put on the purple dress Winn liked

so well. He picked her up wearing his Stetson, starched white shirt, and Wranglers. His boots looked like polished obsidian. When she got in his pickup, she hugged him and sniffed.

He shrugged. "What are you doing?"

"I'm inhaling the scent of you—something else I missed while you were gone."

He leaned down and sniffed her neck. "Aw, I missed your aroma, too."

She giggled. "I think I'm giddy."

"Giddy as in silly or dizzy?"

"Both." She took a deep breath. "You ready?" He nodded. "Let's roll."

***

When they arrived at T-C Quarter Horse Ranch, Andrea's mother stood at the stove cooking breakfast, and her father sat at the table with a cup of coffee.

"If I had known you were coming for breakfast, I would have fixed something special," Carmella said.

The knot tightened in Winn's stomach. He could barely breathe, let alone eat. He didn't speak because he didn't trust his voice.

"Winn, sit down. Would you like a cup of coffee?" Carmella's smile radiated warmth. Dustin Travis sat steely-eyed and silent.

Andrea pulled out a chair across from her father and sat next to Winn. He took a gulp of the hot brew and felt the burn all the way down his windpipe.

Andrea slid her hand down Winn's arm and held his hand. "Winn made it home safely." Her smile turned him to jelly. "Mom, could you sit down for a minute?"

Andrea squeezed his hand. That was his cue. Lay it all on the line. He cleared his throat. "I love Andrea. I would like to marry her, if you approve."

Carmella squealed and hugged her daughter. "I am so happy."

Dustin cleared his throat. "You haven't known each other very long."

Winn straightened his shoulders, bracing for a confrontation. "I've heard of love at first sight, but I never believed it possible until I met Andrea. I know that I love her."

Dustin stood and poured himself another cup of coffee. "How are you going to take care of my daughter?"

"I have a steady job as a lineman." Winn looked into Andrea's eyes and said, "I own the ranch. My mother deeded it to me. She will move out in a few weeks when she marries Sam Howard, and the house will be ours." He met Dustin's gaze. "I already love her. I will spend the rest of my life cherishing and honoring her."

Andrea leaned over and kissed him on the cheek. She smiled. "Sorry, I couldn't help myself."

The door opened and Andrea's grandfathers walked in the house. Andrea bounded out of her chair and hugged them. "Guess what?"

Abuelo grinned. "You're getting married." It wasn't a question.

She hugged him. "Yes, I listened to my heart."

"When?" Gramps asked.

"We're thinking on Veteran's Day."

Turning to Gramps, Abuelo held out his open palm. "I win the bet."

"No money was mentioned," Gramps said.

Andrea's mouth fell open. "You bet on me and Winn?"

Abuelo slapped Gramps on the shoulder. "I only bet on sure things."

Andrea said, "Dad, do we have your blessing?"

He narrowed his eyes, looked at Winn, and said, "You treat her right." Looking at Andrea, a smile spread across his face.

Andrea hugged him, her mother, and both of her grandfathers. "I love you! Now we have to go talk to Winn's mother and daughter. See you at church."

Once they were on the highway, Andrea said, "That was a little tense, but you were so brave. You are my hero."

***

Winn's mother was cooking breakfast when they walked in. Charity sat in the living room watching cartoons. As soon as she heard Andrea's voice, the little girl ran and jumped into her arms. Andrea twirled her around.

"Mom, can we all sit at the table?"

Faith sat across from her son. Andrea sat with Charity on her lap and cleared her throat. "Mrs. Timberman, Charity, I would like to ask your permission to marry Winn."

Charity squealed. "You're going to be my new mommy?"

Andrea laughed. "Only if you want me to be."

"Yes. I want you." She threw her arms around Andrea's neck.

"Mom?" Winn asked tentatively.

"I am happy for you and pray that you will have a good life together."

"We love each other and are committed to give it our best shot," Winn said.

He wrapped his arms around Andrea and Charity. Reaching toward his mother, he said, "Group hug!"

Epilogue

If you would like to read the epilogue of *Light up My Life in Texas,* to discover where Andrea and Winn are one year later, send me an email, and I will send it to you along with the recipe for Andrea's fudgy chocolate cake.

The next book will be the love story between Donald Howard, Faith Timberman's new brother-in-law, and LeAnn Kane, Katie's aunt who plays in the Chicago Symphony. Watch for details on my website:

http://connielewisleonard.webs.com/

Facebook: Connie Lewis Leonard, Author.

Email (if you want to receive the epilogue): rycon70@att.net

Somebody Somewhere in Texas
By Connie Lewis Leonard

You might enjoy reading *Somebody Somewhere in Texas*, published in 2016, which is the first book of the *In Texas* trilogy. Here is the back cover blurb:

Secrets can't be hidden forever. Maybe it's time to pay the fiddler.

Katie Kane fell in love with Brooks Travis at age six. She fell in love with symphony at sixteen. She can't have both. After the unthinkable happens, she follows her dream to Chicago, vowing never to return to Texas. Now her dad wants her to come home. Mom has cancer, and he needs her.

Brooks loves two things above all else: Katie and country music. Together their talent could have taken them to the top of the charts, but she chose Chicago. He heard she got married, probably to some citified, symphony sissy. Brooks is singing for the Lord in the cowboy church when Katie comes home with a son—a son with the same violet blue eyes he sees in the mirror every day. God has redeemed him, but is there any hope Katie can forgive him and their love be rekindled?

Katie's life and dreams are in Chicago. Brooks was her first and only love, but he broke her heart. She can't let her guard down, can't open the gate and let him back into her life. Everything is different now. Well, maybe not everything. . .

For more information, check out the *Somebody Somewhere in Texas* Facebook page.

Available at amazonbooks.com in paperback and Kindle
https://www.amazon.com/Somebody-Somewhere-Texas-Connie-Leonard-ebook/dp/B01N2K9J41/ref=sr

Made in the USA
Middletown, DE
18 January 2022

59006056R00156